This Wasn't Supposed to Be My Story

Defying Expectations, Living My Truth

A Memoir of Resilience & Coverage

Dr. Vanda Seward

Foreword by Linda Villarosa

Dr. Vanda Seward

Copyright © 2026

Advance Praise For
This Wasn't Supposed to Be My Story

People who are incarcerated are human beings deserving of respect, dignity, and opportunities to improve their lives. Dr. Seward's dual "insider" perspective enables her to candidly share insights that are rarely made known to the general public as she bears witness to this premise. Her work has the potential to seed a much-needed culture change in New York's prison system.

> — *Soffiyah Elijah, Attorney, Organizer, Scholar, Advocate, and Educator.*

A searing, triumphant testament to the power of writing your own destiny. Dr. Vanda Seward's memoir is a masterclass in resilience, a raw and unflinching journey from the South Bronx to the highest echelons of criminal justice reform. Her story—of loving a man behind bars while working within the system that held him, of earning a PhD after starting as a teen mother, of leading with unshakable integrity—shatters every stereotype and silences every critic.

With the potent clarity of her mantra, *'I don't give a f,'* she teaches us that true freedom isn't given; it is claimed through courage, education, and an unwavering commitment to justice. This book isn't just a story of survival; it is a blueprint for reclamation. An absolute essential read.

> — *Fox Rich, Oscar-Nominated Documentary TIME (2020), TIME Book, and Director, TIME II: Unfinished Business*

Vanda Seward's life and journey come alive in this remarkable book. As a mother, frontline corrections worker, wife of an incarcerated person, high-ranking justice official, academic leader, and advocate, Dr. Seward has seen it all and brought it all into practice. Now, she brings it to life in print in *This Wasn't Supposed to Be My Story*.

> — *Vincent Schiraldi, Pinkerton Foundation Visiting Fellow, former Commissioner, NYC Probation and Correction*

This Wasn't Supposed to Be My Story is a powerful and necessary contribution to the literature of resilience and justice. Dr. Vanda Seward's life—from her South Bronx roots to her leadership in reentry and education—embodies transformation in its truest form. Her story challenges stigma, restores hope, and reminds us that redemption is not rare—it's possible.

> — *Donna Hylton, Author, Activist, and Founder of a Little Piece of Light*

Dedication

MY GUARDIAN ANGELS

My husband, David

My grandmother, Hortense

Mother-in-law, Nannie

My sisters-in-law, Carole, and Debbie

My colleague and friend Norma

and my best friend, Boobie—

ALWAYS WITH ME

FOR THE PILLARS OF MY LIFE—

My mother, Audrey

My daughter, Tanika

My grandchildren, Chey, Chris, Mikey, and Drew

and my children by Love… Tyra and David, and their
spouses, Jeff and Ericka

THIS STORY IS MINE, BUT IT IS ALSO YOURS

Dr. Vanda Seward

WITH GRATITUDE

This memoir is the result of the support, guidance, and contributions of many individuals. Their input ensured that this work reflects not only my journey but also the broader human experiences it represents.

Family & Friends:

Bruce H., Cheryl I., Chris C., Desire H., Donna H., Jackie O., Kevin M., Lewis B., Roger S., Stacey D., Tanika R., Valerie S., Van C.

Mentors & Colleagues:

Anthony D., Eva G., Feleica R., Fox R., Joseph W., Kim B., Lila G., Lindsey A., Loyce D., Raquel A., Stuart P., Soffiyah E., Victor P., Vincent S.

Table of Contents

About the Author

Vanda Seward is a journalist, storyteller, and advocate whose work amplifies the voices of justice-impacted individuals and their families.

She holds a master's degree in Engagement Journalism from the Craig Newmark Graduate School of Journalism, where she reported extensively on incarceration, violence, and system reform.

Her writing—produced both during and before her graduate studies—has appeared in the NY City News Service, New York Amsterdam News, The Medium, City & State New York, the Times Union, and Crain's New York Business.

She is also Dr. Vanda Seward, a criminologist, researcher, and educator with nearly four decades of experience in New York's criminal justice system. Dr. Seward serves as Director of the Criminal Justice Program and Professor of Criminal Justice at City University of New York, Kingsborough Community College.

Over the course of her career, she has led transformative reentry and public-safety initiatives, including serving as the Statewide Director of Reentry Services for the New York

State Department of Corrections and Community Supervision, Executive Director of the Kings County DA's ComALERT program, and Director of the Kings County DA's Reentry Task Force.

In addition to her most recent MA in Journalism, she holds a PhD and MS in Criminal Justice, as well as a BA in Liberal Arts. Though retired from government service, Dr. Seward remains deeply engaged in advocacy, writing, and research that illuminate the impacts of the carceral system on individuals, families, and communities.

Dr. Vanda Seward

Foreword

As a first assignment for the Feature Writing class I teach at CUNY's Craig Newmark Graduate School of Journalism, I asked my students to write a 300-word essay about a news event – describing what happened and when, how they first found out about it, how it made them feel, and why it mattered. At the end of January 2025, the essays streamed in featuring a familiar scroll of news events, including the murder of Trayvon Martin, 9/11, Hurricane Katrina, and the first election of Donald Trump.

But one essay stood out, at first as a news event that I wasn't familiar with: The December 9, 2024, assault and subsequent death of Robert Brooks, a 43-year-old Black man who was incarcerated at the Marcy Correctional Facility in upstate New York. Four white prison guards pummeled the handcuffed Brooks to death in a brutal crime that was captured on body-cam videos.

The student shared that she had been profoundly affected by the event, recounting feelings of anger, sadness, frustration, and, ultimately, relief -- "the relief," she wrote, "came from the undeniable evidence of systemic brutality and dehumanization, primarily directed at people of color in the New York prison system."

Who was this fiery student, who explained in the essay that the murder of Brooks served to strengthen her commitment to, among other goals, enforce stricter penalties for abusive officers, and promote greater transparency and accountability within the prison system to prevent future tragedies – and how does she know so much about our carceral system? Yes, the students of our university are known to be well-informed and passionate about social justice. But in Vanda Seward's essay, I recognized something deeper, familiar, and knowing.

I would soon learn much more about Vanda, the intense, gray-haired student – closer in age to me than her peers -- who often sat at the back of the classroom, listening intently but commenting infrequently. She spoke up and out only when her younger peers expressed uninformed or naïve opinions, a bluntness I would come to understand as I got to know Vanda better: "I don't care about being palatable," she believes. "I give a damn about the truth."

Vanda has lived more than nine lives, and her memoir examines each of them soberly, with clarity, detail, and empathy. Later in the semester, in a personal essay, I encouraged her to tell the story of her teenage pregnancy at age 16 in the South Bronx. Her account offers a counter-narrative to the well-worn and limited view of teenage pregnancy in Black communities. In the late 1970s, when her daughter Tanika was born, public service announcements blared warnings of "babies having babies" and later, New York City's notorious "shame campaign" would feature sad-eyed, mostly Black toddlers with captions like "I'm twice as likely not to graduate high school because you had me as a teen." Society's view of getting pregnant as an adolescent meant not only a dead-end for the individual but a death knell for the entire Black community.

And the South Bronx, the skewed narrative went, was ground zero for this and so many other problems. Kids having kids were part of the damaged social fabric of the community, at least partially blamed for the empty lots full of garbage, burned-out buildings splashed with graffiti, and empty shells of people, nodding off on street corners. And, of course, poverty. But the real culprit, a history of redlining and lack of opportunity and investment, was largely overlooked.

Vanda offers a different narrative – beyond stereotypes, clichés, and blame. Her big-hearted, full-throated, eyes-wide-open story examines love and loss, books, babies, and a Ph.D., hallmarks of a life thoroughly lived.

Golden Chains Break Too
by ThePoemStory

They said my dreams were too high to chase,

That I should settle, know my place.

But my soul is carved from ancient gold,

A legacy fierce, a story bold.

I carry the voices of those before,

Who knocked on doors and built the floor.

Who turned their chains to stepping stones,

And made the world call them their own.

No walls can hold, no fear can stay,

I mold my future every day.

Through fire and fight, I've learned to grow,

A masterpiece they'll never know.

Author's Note

This Wasn't Supposed to Be My Story is more than a memoir. It's proof that statistics don't dictate destiny—it's a reclamation.

For decades, society tried to write my story for me: teenage mother, high school dropout, public housing statistic. A Bronx girl expected to disappear into the margins. But I refused. I picked up the pen, turned the page, and began drafting a story of my own—one rooted in survival, transformed through purpose, and rising with power.

This book traces the defining moments that shaped me: becoming a mother at sixteen, working inside New York State prisons, marrying a man behind bars, and earning a PhD while raising a family. It is a story of mistakes and miracles, of street smarts sharpened into scholarship, of faith and fight carried through every season. I tell it with unflinching honesty, grit, and grace because our stories deserve nothing less.

I write for every person who has been counted out. For every girl told she'd never make it. For every mother doing her best. For every man and woman behind bars, fighting to come home whole. For every community that is determined to be more than its trauma.

This memoir is about truth-telling. It's about breaking generational patterns without breaking ourselves. It's about love, loss, hustle, healing—and above all, rewriting the ending when the one society gave you doesn't fit.

This wasn't supposed to be my story. But I claimed it, wrote it, and now I offer it to you.

— *Dr. Vanda Seward.*

Preface

The Assignment That Changed Everything

As part of my coursework at the Craig Newmark Graduate School of Journalism at City University of New York, I enrolled in a Features Writing class taught by Linda Villarosa, a Pulitzer Prize–winning journalist and former executive editor of Essence.

Her presence alone was inspiring, but it was her feedback on my personal essay that truly changed everything.

The assignment called for a personal essay with structure and evidence. I returned to a manuscript I had shelved in 2018, a memoir tracing my journey from teen motherhood to coming of age in the South Bronx to a career in criminal justice. I titled it **"This Wasn't Supposed to Be My Story** Although I submitted it late, I eagerly awaited my grade and instructor's feedback.

Professor Villarosa's response?

"You need to write a book."

This Wasn't Supposed to Be My Story— is the unapologetic memoir of my life story, which starts in the

North Bronx–shaped in the South Bronx, as a teen mother who defied statistics to become a nationally recognized criminal justice professional, professor, and advocate. It is a story of survival, resilience, and reinvention that answers a powerful question posed at my retirement celebration: How does Vanda know so much about this population when she is not formerly incarcerated, not in recovery, and not from the hood?

The book traces a remarkable arc—from a Bronx childhood shaped by loss and poverty, through teen pregnancy and the stigma of dropping out of high school, to decades of work inside New York's prison system and later in senior leadership roles shaping reentry policy statewide.

Along the way, I fell in love with and married a man. At the same time, he was incarcerated, balancing the complexities of being both a corrections professional and the wife of someone behind bars. I raised a family, buried loved ones, earned multiple degrees, including a PhD, and built bridges between government agencies, advocacy groups, and directly impacted communities.

This memoir is not simply about my individual triumph. It speaks to the systemic realities of carceral punishment in America—its impact on Black, Brown, Indigenous, queer, trans, and low-income families, and the unfinished work of justice reform. It also offers a deep personal perspective on the intersections of motherhood, love, grief, spirituality, and professional calling. My mantra, *"I don't give a ____"* threads throughout the book—not as defiance, but as clarity: a refusal to be distracted by foolishness, injustice, or wasted energy.

With the urgency of a frontline account and the intimacy of my lived experience, this book will resonate with readers drawn to stories of transformed life experiences that sit at the intersection of where survival under public scrutiny becomes a form of resistance and resilience, by design. It will also appeal to audiences invested in social justice, criminal justice reform, and stories of pushback against systemic barriers.

At its core, *This Wasn't Supposed to Be My Story* is both my testimony and invitation: a call to rethink assumptions about who carries expertise, whose voices matter, and how love and loyalty can survive—and even thrive—inside and outside prison walls.

Chapter 1
Closing One Chapter, Opening Another

Passing The Torch

"I planned my retirement the same way I lived my life—on my own terms."

When that moment finally arrives to consider your retirement, it is an amazing feeling. You look back over decades of work, over all the people, places, and experiences that shaped the journey and the highs, the lows, the unexpected turns you went through.

As I've often said, I have met some of the most extraordinary people along the way, individuals who poured into me and to whom I gave the same in return.

So, when it was my time to end what I call the frontline work, I knew I wanted a retirement party. Now, I do not do surprises well—especially ones I might not like. I cannot fake happiness. So, I reached out to four of my dearest friends—Donna, Missy, Pat, and Stacey. We met at a restaurant in Harlem, where I shared my vision.

My friend Pat thought retirees weren't supposed to help plan their parties, but, of course, I Googled it and proved there was no rule. And even if there had been, anyone who knows me knows I would have done it my way regardless.

I made it clear I did not want a stiff banquet with colored tablecloths and matching napkins, and everyone dressed like they were attending a ball. Because it is not my style, and those events often cost $70 or more per person.

I explained that my guest list would be inclusive. It will bring together formerly incarcerated people, justice-impacted individuals, parole officers, corrections staff, public defenders, parole board members, and more.

I also said I did not want the usual retirement gift of a watch. I have attended countless retirement parties where a watch was presented, yet I have never understood the significance. It simply was not for me.

Most expected that I would not want anything traditional, though a few were surprised. As for my gift, I wanted something lasting: a dedication brick at the Fortune Society's Castle location, a place that has meant so much to me, so that my name and legacy would remain there.

The Fortune Society has long served black and brown people—and everyone in between—caught in the carceral system. Their newsletter was my first real glimpse into prison life, beyond visiting a childhood friend at Arthur Kill Correctional Facility when I was 18. So, when I suggested the brick, my friends thought I was crazy at first. But once I explained the symbolism, they understood.

My involvement was not about doubting my friends; it was about making sure the event truly fit my people.

The celebration was held at a community-based organization in Harlem. We began in their auditorium-style space and ended up on the rooftop. It cost only $35 per person. The food was catered by a former contract manager I knew from FEGS, and the DJ was a man who had been incarcerated and was then working at Exodus.

Dr. Divine Pryor, my beloved brother and comrade, served as the MC. Executives from the Brooklyn District Attorney's Office, New York State Parole, staff from community-based organizations, and formerly incarcerated friends and comrades were among the speakers. Guests included family, to my surprise, my brother flew in from California, along with friends, colleagues, business partners, and allies from the advocacy world. My secretary from Albany Parole Central Office, Lisa, traveled in from Albany, and my childhood neighbors who were once my babysitters from Throggs Neck, Rochelle, and Harriet attended as well. And, of course, the South Bronx crew was there.

Having the crew present meant the world to me. My best friend Boobie, who has since passed, would have been front and center. He had been in the front row at my graduations, and his absence was deeply felt. The influence of the crew has shaped both my professional and personal journey, and they will always remain an indelible part of me.

The evening was everything I hoped for, but one moment stands out most clearly. After the program, Dr. Pryor closed by asking, "I'm not sure if you've ever thought about this: how does Vanda know so much about this population? She's not formerly incarcerated. She's not in recovery. And she's not from the hood." *And that, my dear reader, is precisely the question that will be answered in the pages that follow.*

The audience laughed. What many did not know was that I was not raised in the hood. I was raised in the North Bronx and came of age in the South Bronx—some of my teachers were sitting quietly in that very room. Many also thought I lived within the five boroughs of New York City, where I had not resided in close to three decades.

The laughter in the room, though warm and familiar, was a signal. It was a launching pad, not an end. In that moment, I knew it was time to officially pass the torch, not only of my own legacy, but also of the wisdom and understanding I had spent a lifetime nurturing.

The brick at the Fortune Society stood steadfast as a testament to my dedication. And it was only the beginning. The real legacy was reflected in the eyes of the people who were gathered there. Those people knew my story. They were the ones who had been touched by my work and who would carry it forward.

Everyone was on their feet as the rhythm of Harlem pulsed through the crowd when the DJ spun a record that drew them in. I watched with captivation and content. Justice-impacted individuals shared stories with parole officers, former colleagues laughed with community advocates, and a vibrant tapestry of connection was woven.

I felt a profound sense of accomplishment. This wasn't just my retirement party; it was a celebration of bridges built where walls once stood, of humanity shared across experiences that once divided us. It was a reminder that my life's purpose had always been rooted in lifting others.

Dr. Pryor gave me a knowing smile before stepping back and letting the music and food take the lead. He understood what he had witnessed was my commitment—the way I sought to see beyond labels and into people's hearts.

He already knew the answer to his own rhetorical question. My work wasn't born from circumstance, but from an unshakeable empathy forged through years of listening, of believing in redemption, and of trusting in people's capacity for change.

As I stood there, on the edge of my next chapter, I realized that my journey had been—and would continue to be proof of how one person truly can make a difference.

Chapter 2

Bronx Beginnings

From Coupons to Consciousness in the Bronx

"There was no blueprint and no safety net—just my mother, steady and unshakable, making miracles out of paychecks and coupons. Her quiet fire carried us farther than privilege ever could."

I was born in the Bronx, in the West Farms Road area. When I was about 4 years old, my family relocated to the Throggs Neck Housing Projects, part of the New York City Housing Authority. The move happened following an electrical fire.

I attended grammar and junior high school in Throggs Neck. I spent my free time playing tag, skellzies, Simon Says, jumping rope, roller skating, riding my bike, and hanging out with friends.

I have one older brother, who often acted more like a father than a sibling. He was always trying to tell me what to do, though half the time I ignored him. When I got in trouble with my mom, he would stick up for me. He would also say he would take the spanking for me. That's a good big brother.

We were a small family, part of the working poor, but we held strong middle-class values. My mother became a widow after my father passed away when I was just two. I never really felt his absence because I had no memories of him. My brother, who was five at the time, remembered more.

My mother never spoke about my father—not in longing, not in frustration. She never said, *"If your dad were here…"* or *"If I weren't alone, I could do more."*

Because she never mentioned him, I didn't dwell on his absence. When people asked me what it was like growing up without a father, I never had a clear answer.

How do you miss what you never experienced? For me, it was just another day with my mother, who played both roles.

On Father's Day, we gave handmade cards to my uncle, my mother's brother, but that was the extent of it. My mother never remarried, and to my brother's and my knowledge, she never had a boyfriend—no man ever came to our house. There was never a moment when we had to call some stranger *'Mr.' or 'Uncle.'*

My best friend Valerie's father lived in their home, but I never looked to him to shape my idea of fatherhood. What struck me most was how he cared for his family. He was a man's man—an alpha male—and that left an impression on me about what a man is supposed to do, more than what a father is supposed to be.

My mother was a reserved woman—poised, well-mannered, and composed. You might assume she came from privilege, but she did not. She rarely raised her voice or showed emotion, despite carrying a heavy load. Although she had two siblings, one sister and one brother, she was the most responsible. Many of the elders relied on her, especially during times of loss, when she often oversaw the funeral arrangements.

Despite the pressure, she never broke down. She was also incredibly budget-conscious and religiously clipped coupons. At that time, there were four or five supermarkets within walking distance in Throggs Neck. She would make a list, and we'd visit each store to find the best deals. The money she saved funded our summer camps and vacations.

That habit left a lasting impression—so much that I now avoid coupons entirely. I don't use the word *budget*.

My brother, on the other hand, is the opposite. He still uses coupons and shops sales faithfully. I often joke that I'm "traumatized" by the words *"budget" and "coupon."*

My mother worked for the City of New York and received veterans' benefits after my father's death—he had served in the Army. She was always resourceful and determined to give us the best she could.

During the Christmas season, she took on a second job as a seasonal employee at the E.J. Korvette department store in the Bronx, just to ensure my brother and I had everything we asked for on Christmas morning. Somehow, she always pulled it off.

Holidays were a big deal in our family. Christmas was always at our house, filled with decorations, laughter, and the smell of good food. Thanksgiving was hosted by one of my aunts, and Easter and Mother's Day were spent at my grandmother's. These gatherings were more than meals; they were affirmations of love, tradition, and togetherness. No matter the challenges, the holidays made everything feel whole.

Despite the realities of single parenthood, my mother ensured that my brother and I had a wholesome, rich childhood. We never felt deprived.

I was a Girl Scout, starting as a Brownie and working my way up to Senior—the highest level. I loved selling cookies door-to-door in the projects and even won awards for top cookie sales. Summers were filled with sleepaway camp, day camp, swimming, arts and crafts, and vacations with my mother and grandmother. When I wasn't in a formal summer program, I created my own day camp on the grass near our building, watching younger kids while their parents ran errands.

At thirteen, I went on my first cruise with my grandmother and aunt aboard the Holland America Rotterdam ship to Bermuda and the Bahamas.

Every summer, we took a bus trip with family to Peg Leg Bates Country Club in upstate New York. On Labor Day weekends, I went to King's Lodge with my paternal grandmother (Nana), uncle, and aunt. Both Peg Leg Bates and King's Lodge were Black-owned—something rare and special at the time.

My Uncle Teddy, a Korean War veteran and paraplegic, was known as a "ladies' man." He had charm and style, and he drove some of the finest custom Cadillacs. Outings with him meant fine dining at some of the most prestigious restaurants in Long Island; steak and lobster were a must. By age six, I was eating lobster and linguini in Long Island restaurants, learning how to properly use a table setting and where to place a cloth napkin. In many ways, I was a "princess in training." As I grew older, my world expanded beyond the comforts of childhood.

One of my best friends, Bell, was always getting into trouble. He ended up at Spofford Juvenile Detention Center in the Bronx and later in prison for manslaughter. My first visit to a prison was in 1980, when I went to see him at Arthur Kill Correctional Facility in Staten Island, New York. The journey was long—bus to train, train to ferry, ferry to another bus. By the time I arrived, I was simply relieved to sit still.

Inside, I was struck by the environment: picnic benches outside, families visiting loved ones. I didn't know what to feel. I was just happy to see my friend. We had grown up together. I used to be late for school, trying to make sure he got up and out. He'd always have his tie stuffed in his back pocket, only putting it on at the school door—often too late to avoid trouble.

What moved me most came after the visit. Bell sent me a copy of the *Fortune Society* newsletter. The newsletter fascinated me—not just his poet contribution, but the entire publication. It opened my eyes to the talent and humanity behind prison walls. It changed how I viewed people who had committed crimes. Bell was a good person who made a bad decision. That realization stayed with me.

This experience sparked something in me. I became increasingly curious about the world around me, drawn to stories that explored the complexities of crime and social justice. I read about people like Nicky Barnes, who was considered a crime boss, and the activism of the Black Panther Party.

The sounds of my neighborhood reflected this duality— I remember hearing the voice of the Honorable Elijah Muhammad from the Nation of Islam blasting from a neighbor's window in the back of our project apartment, while James Brown's *"Say It Loud – I'm Black and I'm Proud"* boomed from another window in the front. I loved reading the Sunday *Daily News* Bronx edition. The headlines were filled with the Vietnam War, turmoil in the South Bronx, slumlords burning down tenement buildings for insurance monies, and the rise of illegal drugs and the Mafia.

But my mother wanted none of it in our lives. Anything associated with the South Bronx was off-limits. Drugs, alcohol, and people who lived "the street life" were considered undesirables. She made it clear we were to stay far away.

When my brother left for college in Florida, it was a milestone for our family. I was excited not just for his future, but because I would finally have the bedroom to myself.

Looking back, my childhood was priceless. It laid a foundation that, though shaped by challenges, was rich with love, discipline, and unforgettable experiences.

The ripple effect of Bell's visit to Arthur Kill was profound. It was the newsletter, a window into a world I'd only glimpsed through the sensationalized headlines of the Daily News.

Suddenly, the narratives of crime and punishment felt less abstract, less like distant thunder and more like stories of individual journeys, some tragically derailed.

My mother's firm boundaries about the South Bronx and its perceived dangers still echoed. This burgeoning curiosity wasn't a rebellion against my mother's teachings, but rather an expansion of the values she'd instilled. Her emphasis on discipline, responsibility, and the inherent worth of people, even in the face of hardship, was my compass. I started seeking out stories that explored the systemic issues behind crime and the economic disparities that could push people into desperation. The contrast between the Nation of Islam's calls for pride and James Brown's infectious anthem resonated with this awakening, a yearning to understand the forces shaping lives within my community, both the admirable and the fraught.

The richness of my childhood, while undeniably shaped by my mother's resourcefulness and unwavering love, had also been a protected space. But the world outside, with its complexities and injustices, was calling.

The quiet fire of my mother's determination had lit a path for me. Now, armed with that foundation and a growing awareness of the world's intricate tapestry, I felt the stirrings of a new journey, one that sought to understand the stories often hidden in plain sight. Such stirrings unfolded not on pristine lawns but in the gritty, vibrant heart of the Bronx.

Chapter 3
More Than A Statistic

Mind Your Business

"But being a teenage mother wasn't just a statistic—it came with eyes on me everywhere I went. And in the Bronx, everybody's eyes came with opinions. That's where 'mind your business' became survival."

I officially became a statistic when I got pregnant at 15. It was actually my second pregnancy that year. My mother never spoke about birth control, but she had no issue talking about ending pregnancies.

A few months earlier, I'd had an abortion. There would be no more after that. But there I was… having a baby shower instead of a sweet-sixteen party.

When the news spread, I became the talk of the "town." The whole community was discussing me. Some family members kept their distance, and neighbors whispered behind closed doors. My "baby daddy" was several years older, which only fueled the gossip.

I remember sitting in my room one Sunday, overhearing my mother and a neighbor discussing my pregnancy at the dining table as if I wasn't even home.

When my brother came back from college during spring break, he told me I was having a "bastard child." I had a few choice words for him, of course. I've always had a strong personality and never let people's opinions shake me. But he came home with a new identity—no longer as "Chip," his childhood nickname. Now he insisted everyone call him by his government name, "John." Along with the new attitude came new music—The Blackbyrds' "Rock Creek Park," a song not yet popular in the Bronx.

I sat through my junior high school commencement fighting morning sickness. At my graduation dinner, I spent more time in the restaurant bathroom with my head in the toilet than at the table with my family.

Afterward, I enrolled at Martha Neilson School, a public school in the South Bronx for pregnant girls. As I've said before, the South Bronx was in turmoil. My mother didn't want me there, but she allowed it because at least I was in school.

She worried I'd meet people she considered "undesirable," but her need to keep me from wasting my brain at home, watching soap operas, outweighed her fears.

Going to school in the South Bronx was an education in itself. I learned about the streets, the drug trade, addiction, and poverty. But I also learned how to care for my daughter.

Many teachers told me I was different—that the challenges other young mothers faced wouldn't be mine. Some girls already had two children by the time they turned 18.

I saw firsthand how poverty shaped lives in Black and Brown communities. Even something as simple as baby pictures was a luxury for many classmates. When I became student body president, I organized a picture day so the students could bring their babies for affordable portraits. At school, everyone called me "Big Momma," as I shuffled around the halls in fluffy rabbit slippers to stay comfortable.

One afternoon, while waiting for the bus after school, I met a guy named Boobie. I didn't know then he'd become my best friend. He was five years older, and through him and his friends, I learned about street life, how to carry myself with respect, and how to take no shorts and no nonsense.

I loved school in the South Bronx. I loved hanging out in the hood and soaking in urban life. That time molded me. It gave me lessons I never would have learned at home with my mom and brother, or even in the Throggs Neck Projects. Those lessons changed me.

Boobie became a cornerstone in my life during that time. To think that the guy I met at a bus stop before my daughter was born in the Fall of 1977, we stayed friends for decades. He was like a big brother—mature, shielding, and always full of real-life wisdom to share. Many people believe that people who are street-wise and those who commit criminal acts are not smart, wise, or intelligent, but I learned and saw firsthand that this was not the truth. The crew I was familiar with included college graduates.

I remember hanging out in a game room we called "the spot." One day, my friends and I stayed past lunch, and Boobie told us, "No cutting class in here. Go back to school. We'll be open when you get out." That stuck with me. Boobie and the crew didn't want us skipping class and attracting unwanted attention, and they kept us accountable.

Boobie's mother, Mrs. Chiles, adored me. She used to say, "I don't know why he can't find a girl like you. He always brings those other girls up in here."

When I met my daughter's father, I thought he was handsome. He was from "the Nine"—169th Street and Third Avenue in the Bronx. Back then, if you lived uptown and had a guy from Harlem or the Nine, you were doing big things.

His best friend was also the cousin of my friend Bell, so we clicked right away. He was fun, made me laugh, and didn't mind my sharp tongue. He was five years older, which raised eyebrows, but I didn't care. I was in love—fifteen-year-old love, if that counts.

Even at that age, I wasn't a follower. I was a leader. Nobody could take advantage of me. After my mother forced me to terminate my first pregnancy, I decided that the second time, there would be no termination. This wasn't an accident. I wanted to have a baby. I wasn't following her rules anymore. I wanted a girl, and I never hid that.

When the nurse told me in the delivery room that it was a girl, I said, "That's it. I'm not having any more kids." And I never did.

Being the first among my girlfriends to get pregnant shocked a lot of people. *Not Audrey's daughter, not Chip's sister*. That wasn't the reputation I had. My mother was conservative, and I was known more for being a "good girl" who was respectful and not rebellious. But I stayed true to myself. The comments didn't traumatize me; they just heightened my awareness.

Back then, having your baby's father stick around through pregnancy was a big deal. That was the era of the phrase "baby daddy"—no one said, "child's father." It was simply the language of the time.

Martha Neilson School reminded me I wasn't alone. The way people talked, you'd think I was the only 15-year-old in the Bronx having a baby. But walking into that school and seeing halls full of pregnant girls and young mothers showed me I wasn't the black sheep. I wasn't the outcast. We came from different communities and backgrounds, but we all shared one truth: we were going to be teenage mothers.

The district was committed to keeping us in school and to removing excuses for dropping out. In 1977, Martha Neilson was on the third floor of JHS 136X, off Boston Road and Jennings Street in the Bronx. Climbing those steps pregnant—or carrying a stroller—was no joke. But we did it because we had to.

By June 1978, at the end of the school year, I was transferred to Morris High School in the Bronx. I lasted barely two months before dropping out. At sixteen, with a baby in my arms, I thought I was grown. High school no longer felt like an option.

So, there I was: a teenage mother, a high school dropout, living in public housing, and raised by a single mom. By every measure—and according to all the research—I was destined to fail. My life was supposed to end in disaster.

The same month I dropped out of school, Boobie went to prison. I am sure that had I shared what I was thinking about dropping out of school, Boobie would have advised otherwise. While Boobie was in prison, I looked after his mother. I'd take her to the market, check on her, and make sure she was okay. She used to laugh about her home health aide putting cinnamon in everything—even coffee. "She means well," she'd say, "but I'm teaching her cinnamon belongs in applesauce, not breakfast or coffee."

Shortly after dropping out of school, Bell sent me a package from prison. To my surprise, he sent my daughter a pair of buffalo sandals he made in the prison leather shop. Though they were too small, they sat on my dresser, a constant reminder. Buried in my mind was Bell's humanity, his desire to create something beautiful for my daughter from within those prison walls. This began to soften those edges, planting seeds of a different understanding of who is in prison.

The South Bronx was everything for me—energy, grit, and unspoken rules. Because I learned quickly how to carry myself, the people in my circle knew I could be trusted. I learned that in the hood, you were your brother's keeper. You didn't spill tea, and everyone's business was their business. Loyalty was key to every relationship; you stayed loyal. That's what Boobie and the crew reinforced. The friend circle was small and developed over a period of time, built on loyalty and commitment. This support system went beyond my family. We built an unshakable friendship that still exists today.

Those years taught me more than I could have imagined. I was curious, determined, and ready to figure things out. I knew I had a responsibility to raise my daughter and live life on life's terms. I never felt alone. Every experience became a lesson. It wasn't easy, but it wasn't impossible either.

Coming from a working family, and having friends like Valerie whose family valued work, having a job wasn't optional—it was expected. Even as a young person, I was strong-minded. I knew what I needed to do to be a good mother, a decent woman, and an independent one. The South Bronx showed me that the hustle was real.

My first summer job was at Riverbank State Park in a daycare center. I didn't like working with kids, and the commute from Throggs Neck to the West Bronx was over an hour long. The following year, in 1979, I was assigned to sweep the Bronx Dale Housing Project. I told the summer youth supervisor, "I don't do that kind of work." Because I spoke up, I was transferred to another site—Bellevue Hospital in Manhattan.

At first, I worked in medical records. It was hot, dusty, and by the end of the day, my clothes looked like I'd been playing in dirt. My aunt, who worked in the lab, told me to speak up. I did, and they moved me to the Methadone Clinic—today, in the same building as the NYC Department of Homeless Services' male reception, located on 30th Street and 1st Avenue in Manhattan, New York.

At the clinic, I was stunned. People lined up even before the sun rose—some in suits, others in everyday clothes—for what I thought was orange juice, which I later learned was methadone. That experience shifted something in me. I learned to accept people as they were.

I greeted everyone with kindness, even if I was handing them a urine cup. I saw people as people, many who looked like me, like my neighbors, or like anyone else. Their struggles didn't erase their humanity.

Maybe that empathy came from growing up around people like Poke, a guy who was a heroin user. People referred to him as the "local dope fiend" in Throggs Neck; everyone knew him. Despite his addiction, he still looked out for us kids.

Poke would be standing on the corner nodding, and if he heard us fighting, he'd break up fights and tell us to get our ass down that street to our house. If we did not listen, he would tell our parents. His addiction didn't excuse us from consequences—our parents still punished us. For me, that usually meant no phone and no going outside after school.

What I learned early: people are people. Everyone has a story. And I had mine.

I soon realized my daughter's father wasn't what I needed. I wanted a man who could continuously contribute toward his child's needs, especially financially. About two years after my daughter was born, we broke up. I was only 18, but I already knew I had to hold a job and make sure my daughter never went without.

Thankfully, I had a strong support system. My daughter was the first baby born in our family in nearly 18 years, and because I was so young, everyone rallied around us. My mother, grandmother, aunts, and even my friends' parents made sure she was cared for, had what she needed, and was exposed to the finer things in life.

My elders' attitude was that I was still young and deserved to live my life. Because of that, I never felt stuck in the role of "just a mom." Looking back, I'm grateful I had the chance to enjoy my youth.

Still, I doubt those who encouraged me to live knew I was spending Thursday nights at Pegasus Disco in Midtown and weekends at the 371 Club in the Bronx.

My girlfriend Valerie—my daughter's godmother—and I went to Pegasus so often the bouncer drove us home every week. The only condition was that I stopped and talked to him between dances. Since I knew he liked me, I made sure he bought us drinks.

Although I was having fun in the club scene, I was handling my business. One thing I take pride in is that I never dragged my daughter's father into family court. I managed without his financial help and never spoke badly about him to her. As the saying goes, "If you don't have anything nice to say, don't say anything at all." So, I kept silent. Many have said that was foolish, but my thinking has always been that if the "white man" has to tell a grown man to take care of their children, that is a problem for me. I preferred to leave him to his own demise. There will be a time they will have to explain their actions to both GOD and his daughter.

At that stage in my life, I was drawn to the hustler's lifestyle—fancy cars, sharp clothes, and money in my pocket. I was attracted to men who carried a street persona but were also competent and skilled in their dealings.

By then, I had a strong personality and felt protected by Boobie and the crew. That mix made it hard to be in a meaningful relationship, especially if a man seemed controlling, weak, or not on his game—whether hustling or working a 9-5.

By 18, I had my first full-time job at C-Town Supermarket in Harlem, on 131st Street and Saint Nicholas Avenue. Through my friendship with the head cashier, Debbie, I landed my first apartment in the South Bronx, on 162nd Street and Melrose Avenue. My boyfriend Clancy and I lived together; he was very well-grounded. He knew about the street but was not a part of that action; he was in the military and treated my daughter as his own. Everyone in my family loved him. There was nothing not to love.

As the old folks would say, "He was a good man." But I wasn't mature enough to value him. I had a temper and a sharp tongue. He wanted a family, and I didn't want more children, no matter how much I loved him. We stayed in contact for a few years, and then living life separated us, but we became distant friends. To this day, he holds a special place in my heart. He gave me life lessons I still carry with me.

Working in Harlem in the 1980s was like being in the belly of the beast. Robberies at the supermarket were common, especially during the holidays. I never understood why I wasn't afraid—maybe because I knew the robbers just wanted money. They often came to my register because I'd hand over the entire tray, everything beneath it, and the food stamps, no questions asked.

Even though I worked every day and my daughter was in nursery school, childcare was never an issue. My cousin Stacey adored having "Nik-Nik," as she called her, on weekends. That gave me the freedom to enjoy my teen years. I hung out at The Fever, The Shadow, and Player's Choice. Wherever there was a club or after-hours spot, I was front and center. For me, going out wasn't about meeting men—it was about fun. Dating was tricky anyway. I was careful about who I brought into my home around my daughter, especially.

My first apartment was a one-bedroom on the 2nd floor of a tenement building. The ground floor was a police equipment store, and the owner also owned the building, which made it feel well-monitored and safe. My girlfriend lived on the 4th floor.

The building itself was quiet, though just two blocks over, the neighborhood buzzed with activity. Though small, my apartment was cozy. My mother furnished the living room, my grandmother set up the kitchen, and my daughter's sleeping area was tucked into a corner of the living room.

The kitchen I painted orange and white with matching director's chairs. My bathroom had a gorgeous claw-foot tub, and I stuccoed the walls, which was trendy then. I painted my bedroom tan with a brown arrow design. It was my first place, and I was proud.

I was the first among my childhood friends to have an apartment. I had a job, paid bills, and even owned my own shopping cart for laundry days. I loved the smell of fabric softener at the laundromat; walking up 161st Street with my laundry made me feel grown. Go figure.

When my daughter was old enough, I enrolled her in Embassy Daycare around the corner from our apartment. That's where I met my friend Marion, whose son Calvin was in the same class. Marion wasn't working then and lived nearby, so she often helped by picking up my daughter when I worked late. She'd wait at my apartment, tidy up, and make sure my daughter ate. We became close friends and went out together. She came from a big family and engaged in a lot of activities with her sisters and nieces. She would hang out with me from time to time, and together we made memories. Until today, we are still friends.

I never felt that being a mother was a burden. My family made sure I enjoyed life as a teenager and young adult. With their support, I never thought I had to sacrifice. I could change jobs, go out, and still be a good mother. I always worked to provide for my daughter, and I knew that if I ever needed help—emotional or financial—my family had me covered.

I admired the style of the Harlem and South Bronx crowd around me. Their fashion spoke of confidence; they dressed sharp, even in jeans, sneakers, or sweats. I matched that energy. My clothes and shoe game were tight. I shopped at Fred Michael's shoe store on 149th Street, which sold only high-end women's shoes. You name it—I had snake, gator, and eel heels in every color. During this time, Calvin Klein and Jordache jeans were popular, silk blouses in the summer, and cashmere in the winter. I bought clothes from 34th Street, Lord & Taylor, B. Altman, and Macy's. I even made some myself; my mother had taught me to sew. By 1982, I owned a Louis Vuitton clutch bag. Little did I know I was way ahead of the designer bag explosion.

I was drawn to the lifestyle—the money, fashion, the energy. I worked, dressed well, and expected the same from anyone I dated. If you couldn't come correct, don't come at all. When the crew rolled into clubs like Parkside Plaza, Player's Choice, T-Connection, or The Fever in OJ car #49, people knew we had arrived. There was always a car on reserve—that was a sign of money and power back then.

That environment shaped me. I learned to stay crisp and ready. That mindset never left me.

Boobie was part of every step of my journey. Even when he was away, I wrote or visited to keep him updated. He admired the woman I was becoming—determined and strong.

He was protective. Whenever I mentioned someone I was dating, he'd ask, "Everything all right? No problems?" I'd laugh and say, "No, I'm okay," and he'd answer, "All right, remember, just a phone call away." That thinking continued for decades, even after I got married. He liked my husband, they had friends in common; however, that did not keep him or someone from the crew from asking me if everything was ok, and if "Scrams" was treating you okay.

Boobie was friendly but not overly so. If something went wrong, he handled it. He gave me advice on life and relationships. One of the biggest lessons was about control: act like a lady, let a man be a man, but always stay in control. Never lose yourself trying to follow someone else's lead. That rarely ends well.

Looking back, I realized what I called strength was also survival. At the time, survival felt like power. I focused on maintaining control—never too needy, never sacrificing freedom or goals for a relationship. I cared more about who a person was than what they could give me.

I grew up too soon. I had been around real adults so long that their mindset rubbed off on me. That maturity made it hard to date guys my age—I was too advanced for games and had a distaste for drama. So, I dated older men. It felt easier, less stressful.

I didn't take relationships too seriously. Meeting someone was just that: meeting someone. If I got bored or something else caught my attention, I changed the channel. That was my mindset then.

When I turned 20, my mother bought me a co-op apartment off 207th Street in Inwood, Manhattan, and my daughter and I moved in. She attended the Bible School's pre-K program around the corner. Most of the children spoke Spanish, and her babysitter spoke mainly Spanish with little English, but we managed just fine.

By then, I was working in customer service for the New York Telephone Company. When AT&T acquired it, I transitioned to the telephone store, helping customers set up new service lines or upgrade existing ones. These weren't cell phones—there were only landlines. It was a different era, but the job gave me stability and pride.

I was a professional college enroller. I attended Monroe Business Institute, Steno Institute, Audrey Cohen College, and Orange, Bronx, and Middlesex Community College. Never once making it past the first semester, or should I say, after I received my financial aid check. The truth is, I wasn't ready to commit to education at that time, though it was always in the back of my mind. I knew I would return when the moment was right.

I get bored easily, and that boredom has shaped much of my life. It pushed me to live in 18 different residences across four states and work for 18 employers. I grow restless staying in one place too long, usually after I've already refreshed the walls with new paint and rearranged the furniture. Nothing escapes my boredom.

Relationships don't either. Routine unsettles me. I crave change and spontaneity. I hate gossip and dislike when friends expect me to check in weekly or monthly. That's not to say I avoid real conversations—I'm always there when something important comes up. But I don't want to fill the hours with trivial conversation or updates. I also hate male-bashing. I never engage and will redirect the conversation. I am a strong believer that men do only what a woman allows them to do. The only people I never tire of talking to are my daughter and the person I'm in a relationship with. With my daughter, I might skip a day—usually Sunday.

I've also been a frequent flyer on diet plans—I have signed up for probably every one you can think of. I remember sitting through a diet assessment before starting

Nutrisystem. The counselor told me I would struggle to lose weight because my self-esteem was too high. That was the first time I'd ever heard that connection. There may be some truth to it, because being plus-size has never affected my friendships, relationships, or ability to obtain a job or meet people of the opposite sex.

Even today, my girlfriends and I laugh about men who are strangers going out of their way for me. I have been called a man magnet because men just gravitate toward me. One time, while my girlfriend Pat and I were out to dinner, a man at the bar struck up a conversation with me. The next thing we knew, he had paid for our meal and introduced us to his wife on the way out.

Another time, while having a dinner meeting at a diner in East New York, Brooklyn, a group of city transit workers came in while trying to have the meeting. They grew noisy, and I jokingly told one of them he'd disrupted our meeting and should pay for our food. To our surprise, he pulled out some bills, borrowed a few more from his coworkers, and paid the whole tab.

Another reason is that being plus-size has never been an obstacle—probably because I know how to engage people and always carry myself with confidence and grace.

That spark of spontaneity, the need for something new, always found an outlet, even in the most mundane of routines. While working for the phone company, I'd still find myself drawn to the rhythm of the city, the pulse of its nightlife.

Thursday nights were still for Pegasus Disco in Midtown, the kind of place where the music vibrated through your soul and the dance floor was a temporary escape from reality.

Weekends were for hanging out, hitting the clubs, the after-hour spots, or wherever else the night beckoned. It wasn't about finding a man; it was about the pure, unadulterated joy of movement, of being in the moment. The clubs were a kaleidoscope of sharp styles and confident swagger, and I fit right in. To this day, clothes, shoes, and handbags must be just right. Since I have been prescribed eyeglasses, I had to add them to my list of things that need to be right. Always.

The whispers about my early life, my teenage pregnancy, the rapid succession of jobs, and the constant movement across boroughs and states were all just noise to me. Each move, each new employment, each relationship that flickered and faded, it was all part of the same relentless hum of survival and self-discovery.

I learned to build my own sanctuary, brick by brick, within the chaos of my life. The little one-bedroom apartment on 162nd Street, though small, felt like a palace. It was a space I'd carved out for myself, painted with my own hands, furnished with the love and support of my family. It was a testament to the fact that even when life tried to pin you down, you could still find a corner to call your own, a place to breathe and be still. Even amidst the whirlwind, there were anchors.

Boobie remained a constant, a steady presence through the decades. His advice, laced with the streetwise wisdom of the Bronx, became my compass. "Act like a lady, let a man be a man, but always stay in control," he'd say. It was a mantra I lived by, a silent promise to myself that no matter who crossed my path, no matter what challenges life threw my way, I would never lose sight of who I was.

This fierce independence, this unwavering self-possession, it was a shield, yes, but it was also the engine that propelled me forward, always seeking the next challenge, the next horizon. My thirst for change, for the new, was insatiable. It was the force that drove me from one job to another, from one apartment to the next, from one diet plan to another.

The counselor's words about my high self-esteem resonated. It wasn't about seeking validation from others; it was about knowing my worth, about owning my space in the world. And in that knowing, I found a freedom that transcended any physical limitations. This confidence drew people in, not with neediness, but with genuine warmth and an unshakeable sense of self.

Chapter 4
Running from Myself

Bronx Comes to Cali

"Even with one foot in California, the Bronx never let go of the other. I thought distance could fix things—but the real reckoning came when I had to face myself."

After hearing my brother praise life on the West Coast, I decided to give California a try. My grandmother suggested that I let my daughter stay with her until I get settled in the new job and environment. I agreed, and my daughter started grammar school in Spanish Harlem. She also joined the school band, and my grandmother became a band helper, assisting with the band events. I traveled to California about a month before my move to secure a job at California First Bank on Sepulveda Boulevard, along with an apartment in Hawthorne, California. All of this was handled before I even arrived.

I flew out on my own—young, independent, and determined to make it work. I didn't stay with my brother, though I suspect he expected me to. I went straight from the airport to my new place. That kind of initiative, especially in my early twenties, was something I took pride in. It felt like proof of real maturity.

California had its charms. The weather was beautiful—sunshine nearly every day, with a dry, forgiving heat I've grown to appreciate. I was working full-time, reconnecting with my brother, and exploring downtown Hollywood in my spare hours. Still, something never clicked. The lifestyle felt too slow, too quiet. My brother's world revolved around work, family, church, and bowling with friends.

Meanwhile, I missed the energy, the chaos, the pulse of New York. I came from motion, from noise, from a city that never paused. California couldn't compete.

Soon, I was straddling both coasts. On Fridays, I'd leave work early, catch a 6 p.m. flight, and land in New York around 8 p.m. Eastern time at JFK or LaGuardia. I went straight to the club or after-hours spot, suitcase in tow. Saturdays belonged to my daughter; I soaked up every moment I could with her. Sundays, I boarded the last flight back, just in time to shower and head into work Monday morning. It was costly, yes, but the man I was seeing at that time, a financially stable New York City bus driver, covered my flights.

I kept that rhythm nearly every weekend. Looking back, I see that I never fully gave California a chance. I had one foot in, one foot out. You can't build a life in a new place while constantly flying back to the old one. I wasn't ready to release New York—not my daughter, not my friends, not the city's heartbeat.

After about a year, I knew California wasn't for me. I packed up and moved back to New York, subletting an apartment in the Bronx from an ex-boyfriend, and I don't regret it. California wasn't a failure; it was a lesson. I learned I could leap into the unknown and still land on my feet. That experience gave me more than sunshine—it gave me self-trust and discovery.

But the New York I returned to changed. The war on drugs and the war on crime were raging. Many of my friends from the Bronx were incarcerated or battling addiction. The streets I once knew felt harsher—more dangerous, more desperate.

Looking back, I realize being surrounded by alpha males shaped how I viewed relationships. By the time I was in my mid-twenties, I had already witnessed men who were dominant, reliable, and untouched by the pull of romance. I longed for someone who could disarm me—someone I'd feel safe enough to let into my space, into my craving for something more profound. I wanted joy, ease, maybe even a hint of luxury—but more than anything, I wanted a relationship free from chaos.

Finding someone I truly respected was never easy. I wasn't drawn to long-term commitments that led to marriage or more children. I already had my daughter, and she was enough. I used to joke that if I ever had another child and the relationship ended, when the father packed his bags, he should pack the child's too. I'd arrange visitation and pay for child support.

I was too grown for my age. Being around real adults early on shaped my thinking. Dating guys my age was frustrating—they were still playing games while I was looking for substance. So, I continued to gravitate toward older men. It felt simpler—they were more respectful, financially stable, and far less stressful.

That mindset led me to men who valued independence—especially emotional autonomy. They respected boundaries and didn't bring the chaos I saw my girlfriends endure. I never related to their heartbreak stories. I wasn't chasing men or stuck in nonsense because the men I dated were grounded. Not perfect, but not childish.

Boobie, being older than me, I would look to him if I needed relationship advice; he was the one I called. He wasn't exactly a role model—fidelity wasn't his strong suit—but his advice was solid. He kept me centered. If a relationship wasn't working, I had two choices: walk away or accept it for the season and move on.

Through my late twenties, I held to that mindset. I didn't have short-term flings—five years was usually the minimum. When I was done, I exited gracefully. More often than not, we stayed friends afterward. I avoided emotional turmoil because I kept control. That included my daughter's father. When he no longer fit, I ended it. Did he struggle? I do not know. But I know there was no drama. A childhood friend often reminds me of a time when I pushed him down the stairs and tore the fur off his snorkel coat. I don't recall it.

I know I had a short fuse for foolishness. I was a firecracker—ready to ignite in 2.2 seconds. But over time, I saw how draining that was. I outgrew that behavior, learning to shut things down early rather than explode.

What I called strength back then might have been survival. But it worked. With men, I refused to be dependent, needy, or easily misled. I wanted freedom, identity, and had life goals—and I wasn't trading those for anyone.

In many ways, I was still searching—geographically, emotionally, spiritually—but always on my own terms. Whether it was packing up for California or walking away from a relationship, I didn't wait for anyone else to decide. I definitely was not one of those who did not want to be the first to say goodbye. I trusted myself, even when I didn't have the answers. And that's the thing about growth—it rarely comes with certainty, but it always brings clarity. By then, I knew I wouldn't compromise who I was to keep a man or a friend. And I wouldn't stay anywhere that didn't feel right. That lesson carried me through everything that came next.

Chapter 5
Hair, Hustle, and Home

South Bronx Hustle

"Learning to do hair gave me a skill—but watching the hustle in the Bronx gave me an edge. Together, they became my survival kit."

When I returned to New York City, I was ready for something new. I enrolled at Robert Fiancé Beauty School in the Bronx on the Grand Concourse near Fordham Road. Most beauty students went to Wilfred Academy, directly across the street, but Robert Fiancé had an affluent reputation. It was more expensive and catered to white students. There were a few Black and Brown students, and most of the clients who came in for services were older white women.

Years later, a federal court ruled that Wilfred had exploited its students—mostly young migrants with limited English—in the late 1980s and '90s. The school made their students apply for student loans they didn't qualify for and falsely certified their eligibility for Department of Education funds. I was glad I had chosen the so-called "white people school."

While in beauty school, I styled my mother's hair and Ms. Walden, the neighbor who lived across the parking lot. After graduating, I landed a job at Soul Scissors, one of the first chains of salons for Black women owned by a Black man. Just imagine the "Black Hair Is" movement playing out at an upscale salon on 57th Street and Lexington Avenue, in Midtown Manhattan, in the heart of "beauty row." It was glamor, Black is Beautiful, and our Black crowns meant everything. Weekly, I styled a well-known news anchor, Sheila Steinbach, as well as the wife and daughter of a diplomat from the Ivory Coast, Africa.

I loved the industry, but I wasn't a miracle worker; clients would come in with a picture of a hairstyle. After the hairstyle is completed, they would say it looked nice, but not like the picture. What was usually the problem was that the picture would have either someone younger or of a different skin tone. You go figure how I could assist with that. The long hours wore me down. There was no set schedule; 12-14-hour shifts, and time was money. That chapter didn't last long.

Next, I applied for an entry-level drug counselor position at Straight and Narrow, a therapeutic community in New Jersey. They were launching their first residential program for court-involved youth. I stretched the truth on my application, leaning on my summer job stint at Bellevue Hospital's methadone clinic. My work there had been limited to labeling urine cups and recording basic information, but I made it sound more official. They were willing to train me, and I was eager to learn.

It was my first time working in a drug program as a counselor, and I found it fascinating. Addiction didn't discriminate—it embraced anyone willing to indulge—and the cycle of recovery amazed me. Straight and Narrow was in the heart of Paterson, New Jersey, right in the middle of the hood, and I was working with young people court-mandated to engage in residential drug treatment. Despite the challenges, I felt at home. The energy, the people, the environment all felt familiar, as if I were exactly where I belonged.

That experience pushed me to deepen my understanding of addiction, not just from a clinical perspective but through the lens of the 12-step process. I wanted to speak to clients with relevant knowledge, not just theory. Because I wasn't in recovery myself, I attended an open meeting in Jersey City to listen and absorb. I wanted to know what it meant when I told a client they needed to "go to a meeting."

Those meetings were powerful. They were about conscious thinking, breaking destructive cycles, and owning your choices. And I realized the 12-step process wasn't only for recovery—it was for anyone trying to live with intention. The Serenity Prayer especially resonated: "God, grant me the serenity to accept the things I cannot change, the courage to change the things I can, and the wisdom to know the difference." You don't have to have an addiction to live by that. It became a guiding light, reminding me that sometimes change isn't about fixing the world—it's about adjusting myself, redirecting my energy, and finding peace in what I can control.

Soon after, my daughter and I moved to Edison, New Jersey. We lived in a brand-new three-bedroom townhouse with a big backyard. She went to a great school, far from the urban environment we had known, and that exposure shaped her into the woman she is today. I had already grown used to suburban life back in California—apartment complexes with fitness centers, Jacuzzis, swimming pools—and this lifestyle felt both familiar and comforting.

Unfortunately, I didn't pass probation in the drug program. I think I was too understanding. I had seen addiction up close—the highs, the relapses, the slow climb back—and I knew people needed time.

To make ends meet, I took a seasonal job at the IRS in Downtown Brooklyn. I also worked nights from 11 p.m. to 7 a.m. at Revlon Cosmetics Research Center in Edison, New Jersey, in the department that tested makeup. I thought it was perfect, only ten minutes from home. But by 2 a.m., I was falling asleep, and no remedy kept me awake. I resigned. The lesson was clear: night shifts weren't for me.

Shortly after, I landed a civil service job with New York City's Human Resources Administration as an eligibility specialist and welfare caseworker. When I applied, I claimed to have a GED, even though I didn't. My mother, a longtime city employee, warned me that I had one year to get it before the city found out. I listened. I signed up for a walk-in GED test at Samuel Gompers High School in the Bronx—no prep classes, just confidence. I passed, officially earning my GED in 1984.

But I didn't stay at HRA long. The workload was crushing, and I couldn't wrap my head around grown men showing up at the welfare office with their girlfriend or wife, trying to get a check before I even arrived at 8:30 a.m. It was too much, so I resigned.

I was still in my mid-20s, but I had already tasted life's finer things—vacations, luxury cars, suburban living. I knew I wanted more. Around that time, I bought a two-family house uptown in the Bronx and hired a contractor to convert it into a single-family home. I wanted a sunken living room, dual bathroom vanities, and a tub on a platform—the kind of upgrades you saw in movies in 1986.

The plans were so impressive that my contractor, Tony, an Italian guy, made me a cash offer before I even moved in. I sold the house and kept renting my townhouse. The first thing I bought was a brand-new 1986 Pontiac Trans Am—T-tops, fully loaded, with headers installed. I got a great deal because the salesman didn't believe me when I said I'd be back with cash.

Here's the backstory: I spent the weekend in Atlantic City with my boyfriend. It rained the whole time, and I was sporting natural hair. On the way home, we stopped at a Pontiac dealership in Langhorne, PA. I knew I was closing on the house that Monday. I walked into the showroom looking rough, hair standing on top of my head, but the salesman was kind, showed me the car, and after the test drive, I was hooked. When I said I'd be back on Wednesday with cash, he smiled politely but didn't take me seriously. I had him write the price on the back of his business card.

On Wednesday, I called the salesman and left a message to say I was leaving work and would arrive by six to pick up the car—and reminded him I was paying cash. When I arrived in the showroom, the salesman from Saturday was off, and another salesperson helped me. He assumed I was financing, he quoted me $23,000, but when I said cash, and showed him the $18,000—price written on the back of his business card. The room became quiet.

The salesman called the manager, and soon thereafter, the Saturday salesman appeared. They huddled, but they had to honor the written price. I handed over the cash, and the deal was done. I just hoped the salesman didn't get fired—and that he learned an old lesson: never judge a book by its cover.

That Trans Am was a statement. It drew a lot of attention and eventually triggered severe headaches from the noise coming off the headers. Unfortunately, I had to get rid of the Trans Am. So, I traded in the Trans and purchased a brand new 1986 Mercedes-Benz 190E. Having the opportunity to own and drive such high-end cars was proof that I could create the life I envisioned, even if the road there wasn't straight. Driving the Trans with the T-tops off felt like stepping into my own future. The Bronx wasn't just where I lived—it was where I was building. Something—brick by brick—and I was doing it on my terms.

Chapter 6

Behind the Wall: The Work and The Weight

Beyond the Fence

"Getting the job felt like a win. But once I stepped behind the prison gates, I realized what it truly meant to work in that system. The illusion of control, the silence, the secrets—it changed me.

And yet, I kept going. Even beyond the fences, the job followed me home. That line between professional and personal? It blurred more than I ever expected."

Shortly after resigning from the Human Resources Administration, I began working as a provisional employee with the New York State Department of Corrections. I was one of the first Alcohol and Substance Abuse Treatment (ASAT) Program Assistants at Edgecombe Correctional Work Release Facility, a minimum-security work release prison in Harlem. When I say this was my dream job, I mean it—words cannot capture how thrilled I was to finally work in a prison setting.

At Edgecombe, I learned quickly. The correctional staff was outstanding: friendly, supportive, and committed. Close to 40 years later, Corrections Officer Ivan Godfrey, now Dr. Ivan Godfrey, and I have remained friends. My supervisor, a former nun, was deeply passionate about helping incarcerated individuals. I also saw people of color in executive positions, which was inspiring.

During that time, I joined the New York State Minorities in Corrections organization and served on the Facilities Accreditation Team, which helped Edgecombe earn its first American Correctional Association accreditation. I frequently attended correctional conferences, eager to absorb as much as I could.

One thing I noticed early on was how many people were approved for work release, only to violate their temporary release conditions and end up back in prison. I did not yet understand the concept of recidivism, but I began to wonder what was happening upstate that left people so unprepared for reentering their communities. I was so green about the criminal legal system at this time and did not realize I was entering this arena at the very beginning of the crack epidemic, which led to a drastic increase in people entering the prison system. This was coupled with the Anti- Drug Abuse Act of 1986, which imposed harsh mandatory minimum sentences for drug-related offenses and included a five-year minimum for possession of crack cocaine. Everything happening in the prison system across the country was new because the population was growing rapidly, and programs within the prison could not adequately house or address the needs of the people incarcerated.

After a year at Edgecombe, I met a Department of Corrections executive at a conference. Soon after, I transferred to Orleans Correctional Facility in Western New York, about one hour from Buffalo, New York, where I worked with men incarcerated in a medium-security prison. My daughter and I moved to Cheektowaga, a suburb outside Buffalo. She was the only African American girl at her school and quickly became friends with the only African American boy.

She thrived—skied, played tennis, and embraced a new environment. For her, going to the mall was an event. The friends got around by the mothers taking turns driving them to and from different activities. I worked and did not have time for this foolishness. I would arrange for a taxi to take them where they needed to go. They also did a lot of sleepovers, which was new for me. I never liked sleepovers when I was young, but that was the in thing, so I did not interfere with my daughters' "fun."

My experience was very different. I quickly realized that prejudice was alive and well. At Orleans, I learned that racism was not always about skin color—it was about mindset. Both Black and white staff shared the same negative views about incarcerated people, especially if they were from New York City. If you were from New York City, you were considered the worst of the worst. So here I go into the lion's den. A Black female civilian from New York City who talked like the very people they had such great disdain for.

Despite the challenges, I was able to implement meaningful programmatic changes. One of my proudest contributions was adding a recreational component to the ASAT program to show individuals in recovery that they could enjoy themselves without drugs or alcohol. We introduced group sports at yard time. I remember one summer day while walking the track, when Superintendent Sally B. appeared at the yard gate, upset about "men putting on lipstick and walking around." She was stunned to learn it was me, her ASAT counselor. She could not believe I was in the yard during facility recreation time without an officer escort, which she required because of safety concerns.

I also brought in VHS videotapes with educational or thought-provoking storylines. The men often asked about what was happening in New York City during the crack epidemic—they only caught fragments on the news. I brought in the video New Jack City for a group session. They loved movie days; many admitted they could not recall the last time they had watched a movie sober.

I loved my time at Edgecombe, but my experience at Orleans was equally transformative. I saw firsthand the difficulty of engaging incarcerated individuals in meaningful ways. I also felt the prejudice directed at civilian staff—especially me. I was from New York City, I was Black, and I spoke with the NYC dialect like the men who were incarcerated. That made me a target—but it also made me relatable. I was often asked to oversee programs run by incarcerated individuals and to assist those in solitary confinement with their Tier 3 misbehavior report, hearing evidence.

Because I was well-liked by the incarcerated men, some correctional staff grew uncomfortable. They called me "Snow Black," and jokingly referred to the ASAT peer counselors as the "Seven Dwarfs." I also saw many familiar faces—people I knew from the streets, clubs, or mutual friends. We were often equally surprised to see each other.

One day, while covering my ASAT dorm, I recognized someone—David Seward, aka Goose. After a few conversations, we realized we had mutual friends from Harlem and the Bronx. He was already in the ASAT program and eventually became a peer counselor.

After two years of working at Orleans and visits to Attica and Wende prison, I had had my fill of the prejudice and toxicity among staff. I realized that if I wanted to make a real change, I could not do it as line staff. When I told the peer counselors I was leaving and why, I reassured them I would one day return in a position with more power. They were upset but understood. I requested a transfer to Taconic Correctional Facility, a women's medium-security prison in Bedford Hills. Knowing the correctional officers would make life difficult for the peer counselors I left behind, I added several of them to the transfer list, including David, who was relocated to Mt. McGregor Correctional Facility, just three hours from his home in Mt. Vernon.

My daughter and I moved to Middletown, New York. She loved her more diverse school and being closer to New York City, where she could see her grandmother and great-grandmother every weekend.

My transition to Taconic was smoother because my friend Desire, whom I had met at Edgecombe, worked there as a correctional counselor. I also knew Superintendent Bridgette Gladwin, a progressive warden and member of the New York State Minorities in Corrections organization. But working with women was completely different. The environment was emotionally charged. The women lived in constant conflict with correction officers, both male and female. Often, the female officers were worse—rude and disrespectful.

There was also a great deal of false hope—talk of pardons and clemency that rarely materialized. Some staff even lied to women about their parental rights. The emotional volatility affected everyone.

A few months after transferring, my friend resigned and moved to Florida. Soon after, I went on leave due to migraine headaches, something I had suffered from for years. Stress triggered them. The toxic environment made me feel as though my hands were tied. Any ideas for improving the programming were rejected without explanation. Women considered troublesome were denied sanitary products and toilet paper. Women with children in foster care often went weeks without visits, even when visits were scheduled. The dysfunction was overwhelming.

Having worked with individuals struggling with substance abuse—youth and adults, men, and women, inside and outside institutions—my passion only deepened. Yet I was still uncertain whether this was truly my calling.

The relentless migraines forced me to confront the truth: while I cared deeply, the system itself was crushing me. I realized that true change required a different kind of power. My desire to work in corrections began shifting into a determination to transform corrections.

That was the beginning of everything that came next.

"If you can't figure out your purpose, figure out your passion. For your passion will lead you right into your purpose."—T. D. Jakes.

Chapter 7
Love and Loyalty

Rain, Vows, and Hard Lessons

"Falling in love with Goose broke every rule—and I knew I did. But love doesn't follow policy. What began as unexpected turned into commitment. And on the day I married him—through a downpour, in front of prison green uniforms—I knew my heart had chosen its own path."

While I was on leave, I began visiting David at Mount McGregor Correctional Facility. After several visits and a steady exchange of letters, we fell in love and eventually decided to marry.

At the time, I was still employed by the New York State Department of Corrections, which meant I had to request permission to marry someone who was incarcerated. I wasn't sure how the department would respond, but I quickly realized that if I wanted a future with David, I had serious choices to make.

When I called the central office, I was told—without hesitation—that the department strongly disapproved of such relationships. They made it clear that marrying someone incarcerated could jeopardize my job. That was the turning point.

To help me decide my next move, I brought my mother, my daughter, and my best friend, Desire—each on separate visits—to meet David. I knew he would charm them and answer their questions with confidence and grace. He wore those state-issued green uniforms as though they were designer clothes. He stood 6'6", walked with the ease of a runway model, and carried himself with intelligence and pride. Tall, dark, handsome, a gentle giant, and my husband-to-be.

The three most important people in my life gave me their blessing. I was especially concerned about my daughter, who had a major influence on my decision. For seventeen years, it had been just the two of us. The only men she had known were Clancy, who lived with us, and Adam, her former nursery teacher. If she hadn't approved, I would have postponed the wedding until David came home. But she supported me, and that meant everything.

So, I resigned from the Department of Corrections. In the early '90s, leaving a civil service job—not just any civil service job but one with the New York State Department of Corrections—was almost unheard of. Friends and family thought I was crazy to give up the benefits and job security. But I wasn't worried. I had valuable experience and was confident I could find work again.

Two weeks later, I accepted a position as a supervisor at St. Christopher's Jennie Clarkson in North White Plains, working with adolescent and teenage girls who were court-involved and at risk, many with emotional and behavioral challenges. It wasn't my dream job, but it paid the bills.

While adjusting to my new role, I was also planning a wedding and getting to know David's family in Mount Vernon. The first person I met was his older sister, Carol. When I visited her at the Star Bar and Grill, she greeted me warmly. One thing she said stayed with me: "The family doesn't have any money, but we have a lot of love." And she was right. Everyone was kind, welcoming, and full of love. We spent weekends together and even traveled South during the summers—all before David was released.

I also began building a relationship with his daughter, Tyra, and his three other sisters—Debbie, Gwen, and Jack. Because David's son was still very young, it was harder to connect with him then. By the time David and I were ready to marry, most of our families—both in the North and

South—had already come together and accepted one another.

On Sunday, May 31, 1992, David and I were married at Mount McGregor Correctional Facility. Because he was well-liked by staff, we were allowed a small group of loved ones: our mothers, both daughters, and two of his sisters. Officers were known to say the visiting area was full and limited visits, but not for David. To capture the moment, David purchased about 20 "click-click" tickets so we could take pictures after the ceremony.

Despite the setting, we wanted our wedding to feel joyful and meaningful. I arranged for the family to travel to Saratoga Springs, New York, which was 30 minutes from the facility, the night before. Everyone stayed in a hotel and gathered for dinner—without David, of course. The next day, a heavy rainstorm swept through. Roads were blocked, and trees were down. The staff warned us that the wedding might be postponed. But the rain let up just enough. The pastor arrived, and the ceremony went on.

Because the usual wedding area had flooded, we were moved to the prison chapel during church service. When the congregation was told they'd be witnessing a wedding, the men tucked in their shirts, buttoned them, and pulled up their pants. During the ceremony, David sang "Always and Forever" by Heatwave to me. His sisters joined in, and soon the entire congregation sang along. It was beautiful. Memorable. And filled with love and respect—not just for David, known as "Goose," but for me as well.

As I was leaving the prison, I was handed a brown paper bag filled with handmade picture frames—gifts from David's friends. I treasure them to this day. After the ceremony, the family returned to my home in Newburg, NY, for dinner. The weekend was full of love and connection.

By then, David was more than halfway through his 10-year sentence. Because his case had been newsworthy in Mount Vernon and this wasn't his first time in state prison, he had to be strategic in programming if he wanted a real chance at parole. He assumed we would apply for trailer visits, but that was the furthest thing from my mind. I had worked in a prison. I visited prisons. I was not about to voluntarily sleep in one. I made it clear that trailer visits were not part of the plan. Applying would have required a transfer to another facility. After everything I had done to get him closer to home and into strong programming, I was not willing to risk that.

The anticipation of David's release, though still a year away, became a steady undercurrent in our lives. Every letter and every call carried hope. I began planning his homecoming—simple things: a walk in the park, a quiet dinner, the freedom to hold hands. My daughter, who had grown to love David, often asked about his return.

My days at St. Christopher's provided both structure and perspective. Working with girls navigating trauma and instability reminded me daily of resilience. I saw in them the same fight David carried—the fight to rebuild, to belong, to be whole. Our marriage, born in a place where few imagine love could grow, was preparing to meet the world. We believed in each other. And we were ready.

Working at Saint Christopher–Jennie Clarkson, the girls broke curfew, snuck out, and broke into kitchens or nearby homes. After a few months, I was promoted to supervisor. One day, when I was off, tragedy struck. One girl, devastated by upsetting news from her social worker, set her cottage on fire while the other residents were in the gym. Thankfully, no one was inside, but everything was destroyed—their belongings, even brand-new school clothes purchased just days earlier in the week. The girls had to be relocated until the cottage was rebuilt.

Working with Youth After NYSDOCS (1992)

After leaving DOCS, I took another position with young people at Hawthorne Cedar Knolls in Hawthorne, NY—a co-ed residential facility run by the Jewish Board of Family and Children's Services. I worked with teenage boys, aged 14 to 18, who had been placed there by the courts.

On the day of my interview, I toured the campus. It was striking—almost like a small college, with cottages spread across the grounds, each with its own name. The director, John, a retired NYPD officer, walked me past one of the cottages, introduced it as the "West Cottage," and said that would be my assignment. What he didn't mention was its full nickname—the "Wild West." That title fit all too well.

The boys were relentless. They climbed out of windows to sneak off campus or smuggled girls in through those same windows. In the warmer months, staff sat on the porch at night, trying to catch curfew violators. No matter how hard we tried, little could be done to stop them. Their behavior was reckless—dangerous to themselves and the surrounding community. Some broke into nearby homes, others into the kitchen or gym after hours.

At that time, most of the social workers were neither Black nor Brown, and many struggled to connect with the boys and their families. Cultural barriers ran deep, and I saw firsthand how that disconnect weakened their work and, as a result, affected the young people.

The week I decided to resign to take a position at the Mount Vernon Neighborhood Health Center in Mt. Vernon, NY, my instincts were confirmed. It was a long holiday weekend, the weather was warm, and the boys were up to their usual late-night chaos. This time, two residents broke into the gym. By morning, one of the female residents was found dead. I'll never forget that moment—it cemented my belief that I was in the wrong place. These kids were supposed to be safe, yet they were still surrounded by harm.

That was the turning point. I realized that adolescent residential work was not where I was meant to serve. Looking back, it's clear those young people needed adequate services and resources—things too often denied to Black and Brown youth growing up in poverty. Instead of being protected, they were being failed by the very systems designed to keep them safe.

The sting of those experiences lingered, a constant hum beneath the surface of my new work at the health center. Here, the challenges were different, less about overt rebellion and more about systemic neglect. I found myself advocating for access, for basic health services that were so often an afterthought for Black and Brown families I now served. It was a slower burn; a battle fought in the quiet corridors of bureaucracy. I saw it in the weary eyes of mothers struggling to navigate a complex healthcare system, in the lack of early intervention for children exhibiting behavioral issues that, in other communities, might have been addressed long before they escalated. The same narrative, stripped of its dramatic residential setting, played out in the everyday struggles of poverty and racial disparity. The boys at Hawthorne and the girls at Saint Christopher weren't inherently "wild" or "troubled." They were children in desperate need of consistent, culturally competent support, a support that the systems meant to provide was failing to deliver.

This realization became my compass. My time in residential care, though marked by tragedy and a profound sense of inadequacy, had illuminated the path forward. It wasn't about managing chaos or imposing order within flawed systems; it was about rebuilding those systems from the ground up.

Chapter 8
Coming Home, Building Us

The Road to Freedom

"Freedom was supposed to be a clean slate—but we were still wiping off years of dust. Building a life together meant learning how to live, not just how to survive."

Considering society's biases against people tied to the justice system—and the fact that I had worked inside that very system—I told myself, "I've got to put my big-girl panties on and make things happen for my husband." David trusted me completely. He knew I only wanted the best for him, so I encouraged him to apply for the Industrial Training (IT) program. To qualify, he had to appear before the Temporary Release Committee, which decided whether he could work off prison grounds without being a flight risk.

David's institutional record was excellent, and he was approved on his first try. He joined the IT program, part of Corcraft—the prison industry within the New York State Department of Corrections and Community Supervision. The program gave incarcerated individuals the chance to earn a stipend, build job skills, and take responsibility. David worked in the warehouse and helped with deliveries in the Albany area.

Because of David's lengthy criminal record, I made it my mission that when he stood before the parole board, they would see a man who had done the work and prepared himself for life outside. He wasn't just serving time; he was building a future.

In addition to earning a stipend, he was allowed to go home every other weekend. For about a year, I made the round trip—three hours each way—picking him up on Friday afternoons and driving him back by Sunday evening. There were no excuses, no late returns. We followed the rules to the letter.

Then God called home another angel: my grandmother passed away. She had always believed in me, even when I stumbled as a teenager. She spoiled me, but only if I showed I was striving for something greater. At 24, when I wanted a new Mercedes, she told me, "Save half the down payment, and I'll cover the rest." She loved her clothes, kept her nails immaculate, and taught me to do the same. To this day, I never leave home without my nails and clothing right. And like every elder in my family reminded me, "Never leave the house without clean undergarments. You never know if you'll end up in the hospital." I never wanted to test that theory, so my underwear has always been fresh and in good condition.

I'm grateful she met David and had time to build a bond with him before she passed. Her death shook me. Even though I still had my mother, my grandmother had been my foundation. With her gone, there was no room for error.

David thrived in the IT program. When the state launched a new initiative called Day Reporting, he was immediately considered. The program allowed him to live at home full-time as long as he had a job and reported to the Poughkeepsie parole office twice a week.

By then, I was working at the Mount Vernon Neighborhood Health Center as the social worker for women's services under Carol Morris, the founder and CEO. I had a strong relationship with Mrs. Morris, so I asked if David could work there. I explained the Day Reporting program, and without hesitation, she said, "What day is he starting?"

In September 1994, David began working in the medical records unit at the Health Center. He was thrilled to be home and working every day. I was just as excited, though I dreaded the twice-weekly drive to Poughkeepsie. Still, we did what had to be done.

At the time, we lived in Newburgh but planned to move to Mount Vernon. I had never lived in Westchester, but I believed that if David was going to change, he needed new people, new places, new things. Our relationship didn't need distractions, and one wrong step could send him back to prison. There was no room for error.

I had grown used to suburban living—quiet neighborhoods, space, and privacy. I wasn't used to crowds or having family nearby. But that was David's world.

About six months into his job at the Health Center, it was time for David to face the New York State Parole Board. Imagine this: after living and working in the community, he had to be driven back to Fishkill Correctional Facility, put on his green prison uniform, and sit before the parole board.

It was intense. If they denied him and set a new parole date more than a year away, he would lose everything—his job, his freedom, his momentum. But the board recognized his effort. They saw he was ready. He was granted parole.

When he walked out of Fishkill's gates, smiling widely, he said, "I made it."

That was the end of one phase and the beginning of another. Phase two had begun—the real work was just starting.

We moved to Mount Vernon, and even though things seemed to fall into place, I was still worried. Was David truly ready for change? He gave me no reason to doubt him—no red flags, no missteps—but I believed real change meant changing your people, places, and things.

What I came to realize, though, was that it wasn't just about the external changes. It was about how David viewed those people, places, and things. That shift in mindset made his transformation possible.

As for me, I didn't take shortcuts. I was selective about which of his friends I spent time with and careful about the events I attended. His real friends, Lance, Ben, Ronnie H., Johnny G., and a few others, were what I called real friends; all of them agreed that it was time for David to stop going to the penitentiary. Being from the Bronx, I wasn't part of Mount Vernon's social scene, and some people tried to test me. At my mother-in-law's birthday gathering, I argued briefly with David's children's mother. Someone in the bar who knew me from the Bronx told the people in the bar,

"Goose's wife, she's not just some regular Bronx girl—her crew is a force. Be careful."

Thankfully, that was the first and last time we clashed. Over time, she and I gave each other the respect due to our roles—children's mother and wife. The lack of tension made life easier for everyone, especially the children and grandchildren.

And let me say this: if you think that in your 30s and 40s you can't pursue education or career goals, you're wrong. David's children's mother went back to school and became a nurse. David worked steadily at the Health Center. I pursued higher education. Our transformation didn't just benefit us; it rippled out to our children and grandchildren.

At that point, my husband's freedom was everything. My focus was on him and my daughter. Everything else was secondary.

Still, the stress of worrying about David's future— though self-inflicted—was real. He never gave me a reason to doubt, but I couldn't help it. To stay balanced, I needed a goal or activity of my own. I did not want to worry about the depth of my husband's seriousness about not going back to prison. His actions and decisions were totally under his control, not mine. So, I enrolled in college. My daughter was in high school, and it felt like the perfect time.

I went to speak with my CEO, Carol Morris, who encouraged me. She said, "Four years will pass whether you're in school or not. You might as well have something to show for it." She was right.

I enrolled at the College of New Rochelle, School of New Resources, for a B.A. in liberal arts. My family supported me completely. I went to school at night twice a week, and David and my daughter took turns cooking—or, should I say, ordering dinner.

During this time, David's parole officer, Whitehead, became a trusted ally. He admired David's progress, often saying, "I wish I had a whole caseload of people like you—determined to change."

PO Whitehead even approved our first family road trip to Florida. The only condition: David had to check in with the sheriff's department in Kissimmee when we arrived and again when we left. Each time we appeared at the sheriff's office, both sheriffs looked at us like we were crazy because they had never heard of anyone having this type of requirement. Me being me, I had them write the date and time on their business cards as proof we were at the sheriff's office. When we returned and gave the business cards to Officer Whitehead, he laughed and said with a sound of disbelief, "You really went to the sheriff's office." It had been a test—and we passed.

By then, David had become a grandfather. His daughter Tyra gave birth to her daughter Chey, and he worked hard to build a strong bond with them. His son was in his last year of high school, and they were reconnecting, too. David hadn't been present for much of their youth, which left wounds on all sides, but together we learned that you can't reclaim time—you can only move forward, with no regrets. As my sister-in-law Debbie always said, "If you knew better, you'd do better."

Around the same time, my daughter became pregnant with her first son, Chris. David had to come to terms with being a grandfather twice over. He embraced the title and looked forward to being their Papa.

After nearly two years on parole, David finally braved his first airplane flight and earned his wings, given by the airplane crew usually given to the children. We went big— we went to Hawaii. The 20-hour trip was daunting, but once he landed in Honolulu, he was in awe. He climbed Diamond Head, attended a luau, and stood on the black-sand beach.

We even island-hopped to the Big Island and had lunch in Hawaii Volcanoes National Park restaurant, The Rim, which is located on the rim of Kilauea Caldera, an active volcano. It was the trip of a lifetime.

With his fear of flying gone, our next adventure was a family trip to Florida and Atlanta. We took all our children, the grandchildren, and my mom on an all-expenses-paid vacation. We went to Disney, toured Universal Studios, and then drove to Atlanta to visit the new Martin Luther King Jr. museum. It brought our blended family closer together. Mission accomplished.

As the children grew older, we started taking adult vacations with them— joining them for dinners, dancing, lounges, and simply enjoying each other's company. We were the "cool parents," and we had fun—no judgment, just love. Despite all the horror stories I had heard about in-laws and blended families, we never had issues. Everyone got along.

The freedom David had worked so hard for began to bloom into a life I'd only dared to dream of for us. He continued at the Health Center, his steady presence a comfort to me and a testament to his commitment. My college coursework was challenging, but the intellectual stimulation was a balm for the anxieties that still lingered beneath the surface. Seeing our children and grandchildren thrive, building new memories and forging stronger bonds, filled my heart with a quiet joy that resonated deeper than any past hardship. It wasn't just about surviving; it was about flourishing, individually and as a united front.

David's journey was a powerful example of transformation, not just in actions but in spirit. He embraced his role as a grandfather with a tenderness that was deeply moving, showering his grandchildren with the affection he hadn't always been able to give his own children. His son, now a young man, was finding his footing, and the father-son conversations became more frequent, more open. I watched them, with a lump in my throat, witnessing the healing that was taking place, the slow mending of what had been broken. This, I realized, was the true essence of freedom – not just the absence of bars, but the presence of connection, love, and a genuine peace.

As we navigated these years, the world outside our home continued to present its challenges. There were still whispers, still judgmental glances, but they held less power now. Our lives were a testament to resilience, to the unwavering belief that people could change, that second chances were not only possible but often transformative. We had built a fortress of love and support, a sanctuary where forgiveness was a given and growth was a continuous endeavor. The road to freedom had been long and arduous, but standing on its firm ground, hand in hand with David, with our family surrounding us, I knew every single step had been worth it.

Names and Memories

The weight of the world, or at least our small corner of it, felt like it had lifted with David's parole. But the real work, as I noted, was just beginning. Our move to Mount Vernon was a deliberate, conscious effort to weave David into a new life. I recognized my own suburban comfort and the subtle anxieties that came with stepping into his familiar world. It wasn't just about changing his external environment; it was about the internal shift in how he perceived and engaged with the people, places, and rhythms around him. I was going through my own transition as well, learning to navigate the social intricacies of Mount Vernon, a stark contrast to my Bronx roots, and learning to establish boundaries without resorting to the aggression some expected.

During my time at the Mount Vernon Neighborhood Health Center's Homeless Services Unit—a mobile clinic serving Westchester residents, living in hotels across Westchester and New York City—some moments reminded me exactly why this work mattered. The days were a constant ebb and flow of human stories.

One was Dana, a woman who had been unhoused for years and was well known to residents, case managers, and medical staff. Her passing at a hotel in the Bronx was not just a loss—it was a reminder of how long-term displacement wears on the body and spirit. I believed her life deserved to be acknowledged. I arranged a memorial service at Camelot Funeral Home in Mount Vernon. Ms. Valentine, the funeral director, allowed us to host a two-hour service at no cost. People came from across the Bronx and Westchester to honor her. We even learned she had a daughter. It reaffirmed my belief that when the death angel visits, we must honor the journey, no matter how difficult or marginalized it may be.

Another moment that stayed with me happened at the Cross County Motor Inn in Westchester. An unhoused woman who knew me before she was displaced always greeted me when our mobile unit arrived. She would share updates about her life and her plans to move forward. One day, now pregnant, she rushed down two flights of stairs so she wouldn't miss seeing me. At the last step, her water broke. EMTs were called, and she gave birth during transport to the hospital. Later, I learned she named her daughter after me—Vonda, spelled V-O-N-D-A. I was shocked, humbled, and deeply honored. I hoped the name would serve as a reminder of our conversations—of encouragement, empowerment, and the belief that change was still possible. She eventually moved into her own apartment and, to my knowledge, is still doing well.

These moments—of loss and of life—are the heartbeat of my work and advocacy. They remind me that our work is not just about systems or services. It is about bearing witness, honoring humanity, and leaving behind something more than paperwork: a legacy of care.

The years that followed were a testament to this. David's transformation was not sudden but gradual, nurtured by steady effort and his commitment to freedom. He found purpose in his work; I found intellectual renewal in my college studies. Our children and grandchildren became the vibrant threads of our blended family. Vacations, dinners, and simple conversations were not just moments of joy, but affirmations of resilience and love. We were not just building a life. We were building a legacy—one rooted in healing, redemption, and the unwavering belief that a beautiful future was always within reach.

My Awakening

The constant hum of progress, the rhythmic beat of a life rebuilt, was now the soundtrack to our days. David's unwavering commitment to his parole conditions, his dedication to his work at the Health Center, and his growing presence in his children's and grandchildren's lives painted a picture of a man finally at peace. My own academic pursuits, the late-night studies fueled by Twizzlers strawberry licorice and determination, were more than just a personal goal; they were a quiet act of defiance against the limitations that society often imposed, a testament to the fact that growth knows no age or circumstance. We were a testament to God's work and the power of perseverance, a living embodiment of the belief that redemption wasn't just a concept, but a tangible reality forged through hard work, unwavering love, and a steadfast refusal to be defined by past mistakes.

Yet, beneath the surface of this hard-won serenity, a different kind of journey was unfolding within me. The spiritual influences I had encountered, from the powerful sermons of Bishop Jakes to the disciplined devotion of Minister Farrakhan, began to stir something profound. It wasn't just about finding comfort or guidance; it was about a deepening understanding of my own purpose. The quiet conviction that had fueled my efforts to build a new life for David was now transforming into a bolder, more resonant purpose. The lessons I had absorbed, the empathy cultivated through years of working with vulnerable populations, and the deep wells of faith I had discovered were converging. I recognized that the resilience I had championed in others was also a profound spiritual strength within myself, a gift I was now ready to share more openly, not just through my actions, but through my voice. The road to freedom, I was learning, was not a singular destination, but a series of awakenings, each one leading to a deeper understanding of who I was meant to be and the impact I was destined to make.

Two years into my academic journey, I experienced an awakening—about life, about how I wanted to shape myself, and about the values that would guide me. It began when I first heard Erykah Badu's debut album Baduizm in 1997. Her song "Apple Tree" struck a chord with me:

"I pick my friends like I pick my fruit.

I don't walk around trying to be what I'm not.

I don't waste time trying to get what you got.

I work at pleasing me because I can't please you."

Those lyrics have stayed with me for more than 28 years. They let me live my life on my own terms and reminded me to stay rooted in who I am. Along the way, I began collecting quotes that carried me through different seasons of my journey: "Dare to be brilliant." "Dreams are real." "Never bought or bossed." "You have to meet people where they are—and sometimes you have to leave them there." Quotes became anchors for me, reminders to stay steady. And through it all, my faith in God kept me grounded, always providing the tools I needed for the road ahead.

I don't quote scripture often, nor do I speak openly about religion, because I still consider myself a student of God—I am learning every day. To God be the glory. Over time, I have followed and learned from several religious leaders whose teachings deepened my walk. Bishop T.D. Jakes, Joel Osteen, and Creflo Dollar, among others, each offered me messages of strength, growth, and perseverance that I continue to carry with me.

I remember organizing two faith-based forums while working at the Brooklyn DA's Office. One was a reentry symposium at the Marriott Hotel downtown Brooklyn, where I invited several clergies whom I had met through my criminal justice work. At that event, two of my girlfriends—

former colleagues—overheard someone say, "I know all these clergy, and I don't even go to church." One of my girlfriends quickly corrected them, saying she often called me on Sundays, and I was either on my way to church or just returning. That moment reminded me how little I share that side of my life. I don't volunteer the information, but if asked, I'll answer.

Another time, I organized a mentoring workshop with Prison Fellowship Ministries in Brooklyn. During that session, a clergy member I didn't know told me he had received a message that "greatness awaits you" and that one day I would teach the Word. I didn't embrace it openly then, but it stayed with me. Shortly after, Reverend Jones, a minister friend and former colleague, told me that I was already ministering every day through my work in the criminal justice space.

My spiritual influences are broad, and my quest for spiritual knowledge has led me to Detroit several times to hear the Honorable Minister Louis Farrakhan speak during the Nation of Islam's Saviours' Day commemoration, which honors the birth of Master Fard Muhammad. Minister Farrakhan's words of wisdom and truths have also helped me grow spiritually as a leader—his lessons and teachings are powerful.

My interest in the Nation of Islam deepened after meeting my friend Shawn in Buffalo. He has five sons and two daughters, all of whom are faithful followers of Islam. His sons are members of the Fruits of Islam—the FOI, the paramilitary wing of the Nation of Islam. Their discipline and purpose moved me. To see young Black men so committed, disciplined, and faithful—in a world where that is increasingly rare—left an impression. Today, they have grown up with families of their own, passing down the same discipline and devotion to their children. That, to me, is powerful.

Chapter 9
New Roots, New Rules

Goose's House, My Rules

"Moving to the Poconos wasn't just a change of scenery—it was my declaration. This was his house, my rules, and a peace we created from everything we had survived."

As soon as David completed parole, we bought a house in Long Pond, Pennsylvania, in the Poconos. I was relieved not to renew our lease in Mount Vernon; it felt like I had been paroled, too. David was ecstatic. We must have toured at least thirty houses before choosing the one we wanted.

When we were house hunting, David only cared about one thing: the backyard. He never asked about the layout, bedrooms, or kitchen. I used to joke, "Are you planning to sleep outside?" But it was part of his plan. He wanted a big yard for big barbecues—and that's exactly what we had.

Every year, we host a massive barbecue with at least a hundred guests. Cars lined the street, filled our driveway, and blocked some of the neighbors' driveways, too. We had no choice but to invite all our neighbors within a mile because the music was loud and the crowd was large. David loved those gatherings. It was his way of celebrating life, family, and the freedom he cherished. He invited everyone he loved to enjoy a day at "his house." He was so proud to be a homeowner.

There were rules, though. If you came to our house for an event, you came empty-handed—we had everything you could need. The only exception was for the card players: if you wanted to play cards, you brought money. If you didn't want to gamble, you didn't play. Needless to say, everyone came prepared. The dice players were in the shed. The Seward family was known for playing cards and gambling.

I was still very particular about who entered our space. I asked David to handpick the guests. One year, a woman he grew up with showed up uninvited. She said she'd heard about the cookout and drove nearly two hours to surprise him. When she rang the doorbell, I answered. She asked for "Goose," not knowing who I was. I introduced myself as his wife, pointed her toward him, then pulled him aside to ask if he knew she was coming. He said no—someone else must have told her.

Because my home is sacred and I do not believe in uninvited guests, I pulled her aside and explained that this was an invitation-only event. I asked if she needed the restroom and offered her a plate to go. She was shocked. She explained how she knew David, and I did not doubt her, but she was not invited, so she had to leave.

My family thought I was being extreme, but I wasn't. I controlled who entered my space. I've been told I'm not always the friendliest person—and situations like that justify my protectiveness over my husband, my home, and our life. Besides, who drives two hours without an invitation?

Because David had spent so many years incarcerated, he had lost the spirit of Christmas—and other holidays. I made it my mission to bring that joy back. Holidays became a big deal in our household, especially at Christmas. With so many sisters, in-laws, nieces, nephews, children, and grandchildren, we had to start shopping early—and always in bulk.

I wanted David to experience everything he had missed. Since we could never figure out what to buy each other or how much to spend, we started a tradition: we'd write dollar amounts on slips of paper, toss them into a hat, and draw to set our gift budget. Of course, we never stuck to it—we always spent more. I was the simpler one; David often relied on my daughter for gift ideas. I'd look at what he needed or just ask him. He was easy to please, and he made even simple gifts feel extravagant because he appreciated every bit of love he received— from Nika and the boys, to Tyra, David, and their children.

Greeting cards were serious business and were something instilled in me from childhood, something I still take very seriously—no humorous cards allowed. They had to say exactly what we felt or needed to hear. Every year, the cards David gave me became more heartfelt, more intentional.

As time went on, we scaled down Christmas a bit. But we always made sure the grandkids and their parents had something from us. Christmas was brought in at Tanika's house, and no matter what, we made our rounds on Christmas Day—brunch at one house, lunch at another, dinner at a third. By the end of the day, we had seen all our immediate family.

David loved being with his kids and grandkids. He was the one who enjoyed attending sports games for his grandsons, picnics, and sitting under the tree with family. Those weren't my things. I do not like sporting events or picnics. When I am not traveling, my favorite pastime is shopping, and David developed the habit as well. We had fun shopping together. We'd visit all the stores, have lunch or dinner, then come home and try everything on, turning it into our own little fashion show. We both took pride in dressing well.

Due to the demands of my job as the Executive Director of a forensic program in lower Manhattan, we sold the Pocono home and purchased a home in New Jersey, and we continued the barbecue tradition and added hosting Thanksgiving dinner. Our Thanksgiving gatherings typically drew over eighty people. Before dinner, we'd go around the room sharing why we were thankful. That alone took about forty-five minutes. David loved it. He didn't care that it was cold outside. He'd be out there supervising me, frying turkeys in a winter hat and gloves, smiling the whole time.

Sometimes my sisters-in-law would stay over, and we'd get up early for Black Friday. I'll never forget David's first experience with Black Friday. We were living in Pennsylvania, and my daughter and I woke him up at 3:00 a.m. to go to the Tannersville outlet to catch the early bird sales. He thought we were crazy—but he came. From that day on, for nearly twenty years, we never missed Black Friday. David was always there, carrying all the bags and getting his shopping done as well.

Eventually, my daughter's girlfriend, Tameika, joined us, and we'd make an entire day of it. David would shake his head in disbelief as we shopped for hours without stopping to eat. He didn't love chaos, but he was a trooper—always there, helping us carry the load. The sheer volume of Black Friday bags became a running family joke. David, ever the steady observer, would end up with an armful and a smirk, asking, "Are we done yet?" Even with the playful complaining, his eyes always held something warm—he enjoyed seeing us happy. Participating was his way of reclaiming ordinary joy; the kind of joy prison tries to steal.

Our holidays were a carefully curated blend of David's desire to relive missed moments and my instinct to create order and celebration. The house—which I called "Goose's House, My Rules"—became a sanctuary. Each barbecue, each Thanksgiving, each Christmas, was a testament to our ability to build a life brick by brick, filled with laughter, love, and the occasional, highly anticipated, card game.

And so, the seasons turned, marked by the rhythmic pulse of our shared life. The Poconos became more than just a house. It was the stage upon which we painted our new reality—a canvas splashed with the vibrant colors of family, friendship, and the unwavering strength of our bond. David, having finally found his footing, reveled in the everyday magic: the roar of the grill, the sound of grandbabies running around up and down the stairs. Christmas morning joy, all within the safe and sacred walls of his house—under our rules.

Motorcycles and Alpha Riders Motorcycle Club

While continuing to reinforce my foundation as Mrs. Vanda Seward, Goose's wife—advancing in my career and hosting family gatherings—I also returned to another love of mine: motorcycles. I had ridden with two of my exes, Adam and Sonny, when I was younger, but in 2007, I became an Alpha Rider—a motorcycle club out of East New York, Brooklyn. My biker name was Rotten, which was very fitting because I was spoiled and everyone knew it.

The Alpha Riders aren't just a motorcycle club. They are a community. The membership included elected officials at all levels of government. Brooklyn's last two or three district attorneys have been Alpha Riders. At one point, the NYPD police commissioner was an Alpha Rider, too. It's a different vibe—not an outlaw club, but a club that poured back into the East New York Community. They host toy and coat drives, as well as support community programs for families and kids.

The president, Mr. B, also runs the Alpha School in East New York, which helps young people earn their GEDs when the mainstream system has failed them. Many of the students are gang-affiliated, but inside the Alpha School, they're just students with a common goal: "Get that GED." Gang Colors mean nothing in the Alpha space. No security guards or surveillance cameras, just "Mr. B" holding it down.

I decided to get my motorcycle license and signed up for a three-day class. On the last day, if you passed the road test, you simply took your paperwork to the DMV to get your license. I did it in one weekend. Everyone was surprised that I got licensed in three days. The very next week, I bought my first bike—a Black 2008 Honda Classic 1600R, dressed in purple lights.

I rode everywhere—to the mall, to the outlets, all over town. Speed was my thing. I remember one year when the Alpha Riders hitched up the bikes and rode down to St. George, South Carolina. Around two in the morning, we jumped on I-95, riding nearly 140 mph in a no-helmet state. The sky was clear, stars overhead, and we were tearing up the road. Everyone was shocked that I was such a strong rider as a new rider. I had no fear; going down (falling) was part of the biker life. I've gone down twice with no major injuries.

One day, Mr. B rode to my home in New Jersey, thinking he would help me get comfortable riding on the highway. He never asked if I had been on the highway yet. We jumped on Interstate 280 West in New Jersey, and I left him. He was trying to catch up; he was in shock that I could ride that well.

Later, I sold that bike and bought a 2018 Suzuki Boulevard, though I didn't ride it much because I developed carpal tunnel in both hands. The love for riding had me considering an electric trike, but then in 2024, I was diagnosed with vertigo and had to give up riding altogether.

Riding a motorcycle is an experience you can't explain. People are always surprised to see a woman riding. On the highway, kids would point it out to their parents because they could tell I was a woman. In the summer, I wore cut-out gloves, so my nails showed. Once in St. George, South Carolina, when I got off the bike, people froze—they could not believe a woman had been the one riding. I could even ride in stilettos—not often, because it was uncomfortable— but I did it. I fell a few times, but I always got back up and rode again. That's a sign of a true biker.

David was an Alpha Rider member too, bless his steady heart; he drove his truck, his presence a constant. David never rode with me, but he would follow in the truck with the other SUV members when the club traveled. The thrill of speed and the freedom of the ride were all mine.

But the road, much like life, has its twists and turns. Mine eventually led me away from the roar of the engine and the wind in my face. The vertigo, a cruel trickster, grounded me. Yet even in stillness, the spirit of Rotten remained. The sense of community and shared purpose that pulsed through the club stayed with me.

Although my busy schedule does not allow me time to engage in the Alpha Riders' activities, I am always watching and cheering from the sidelines as Mr. B and the others continue their work, toy drives, coat drives, and programs designed to lift those who need it most. It was a legacy I was proud to have been part of, even if I could no longer lead the pack. Even when I wasn't on two wheels anymore. David understood the freedom, without craving the speed. He saw the dedication of the Alpha Riders, the way they navigated Brooklyn, not for show, but for service.

The sting of giving up my bikes never faded, but the exhilaration, the belonging, the memories remain indelible. My friendship with Mr. B, aka Barry Addison, is a true bond that has evolved and is built on care and concern, which can never be broken. He's one of my biggest supporters and one of my few ride-or-die friends. The open road may have been closed, but my path to community and purpose never was. My spirit—my Rotten spirit—was always built to ride.

Chapter 10
Books, Babies, and PhD

Degrees of Transformation

"Going back to school felt like chasing the impossible. But each degree wasn't just for me—it was for every 'girl like me' who never got the chance. And along the way, I kept getting those calls—reminders that my journey wasn't just mine. It was theirs, too."

Time flew, and before I knew it, it was May 1999. I was preparing to graduate from the College of New Rochelle School of New Resources with a Bachelor of Arts in Liberal Arts. My major was social science, and my minor was psychology. I graduated with honors. I had worked hard, taken school seriously, and the support I received from David and the family was overwhelming.

There were times I missed family events, and even on trips down South for reunions, I would be in the hotel room finishing a paper or wrapping up homework. But I loved the journey. Those four years were challenging yet rewarding— enough to convince me to keep going. I told David I wanted to pursue a master's degree. His response, as always, was simple and supportive: "OK, Boo." That fall, I began my master's program. I attended John Jay College, but I was not accustomed to such a large college environment, so after one semester, I transferred to Iona College in New Rochelle. That was what I needed: a more personable college experience, and I received a partial scholarship as a result of my undergraduate GPA.

One of the biggest lessons I learned during my academic journey was how to juggle work, family, and school. To stay balanced and reduce stress, David and I made it a rule to take a vacation every 90 days. Whether it was a long weekend, a four-day getaway, or a full week—with schoolbooks and laptops in tow—we made it happen. Since we both worked at the Mount Vernon Neighborhood Health Center, getting time off was never an issue.

We loved going to San Juan, Puerto Rico. It was close, affordable, and felt like a second home. We went so often that some locals thought we lived there. We took public transportation and rarely rented a car. We also loved cruising, and we went on so many that I eventually started organizing group cruise trips so family and friends could join us. We had a blast and cherished sharing those moments with family and friends.

Sometimes we would hop in the car with our dog, Tigger, and drive to South Hill, Virginia, or Maryland for a few days to visit family and to relax. Most of the time, no one even knew we were gone until we returned. No permission is needed.

David and I enjoyed many of the same vacation activities—jet skiing, sightseeing, relaxing on the beach, and exploring local towns. There were only two things he didn't enjoy that I did: scuba diving and visiting local jails. In every country we visited, I tried to see the jail. It was something to which I was simply drawn.

Too Good to Be True

Our relationship was built on mutual respect and maturity. We didn't curse at each other, call each other out of our names, or slam doors. We didn't do the silent treatment. That's not to say we didn't get on each other's nerves—we did—but respect kept us grounded. That was our way for nearly 31 years, and it worked.

People often thought our relationship was too good to be true. Some even tried to stir things up. I recall one day at work at the Health Center when I received a call from a woman upset because David hadn't helped her fix her car during his lunch break. She said he was in the car with another woman from the Health Center and wouldn't stop to help. I couldn't understand why she was calling me; I wasn't in the car. I offered to transfer her to the woman he was with, but she declined.

As the call went on, I realized I wasn't giving her the reaction she wanted. So, I said, "I understand. I'll sell my house, my fur coats, and stop going on vacations with my husband because he didn't help you fix your car. I hope that satisfies you." She hung up and never called again.

Let's be clear—David wasn't a saint. About six years into our relationship, he had a brief affair with a young receptionist at the Health Center. By then, I was no longer working there. I had earned my degree and was working in New York City as a Director at Federation Employment Guidance Services (FEGS), one of the largest nonprofit behavioral health agencies at the time.

Ironically, it was a woman I had gone to school with and later hired who told me. She thought David was seeing her best friend and didn't want it to affect her job, since I was her supervisor.

After confirming the affair with her best friend, I called my friend Boobie. I told him what I had learned, and he gave me advice: "Stay calm. Don't yell. Don't scream. That's what men expect. When you stay calm, it makes us nervous. Makes us think you've got something up your sleeve."

So, I followed his advice. I approached David calmly. He thought I was going to end the marriage, but I told him it would take more than that. I did, however, make one thing clear: "If you need a side chick, make sure she has a good job, one that can help you pay some of these bills. I don't need you taking care of her." We had just purchased the house in Pennsylvania. If someone were going to leave, it would be me. I was not about to be stuck with the bills. Even after that incident, there was no drama. No yelling. No screaming. I didn't have time for foolishness. I was working full-time, going to school full-time, and trying to push forward with phase two of my criminal justice career.

At that time, we were still living in Pennsylvania. David commuted to Mount Vernon every day, and I commuted to Lower Manhattan. Most of our time was spent on the highway, traveling to and from work. The commute wasn't ideal, but we stayed focused. We knew why we were doing it—we had a beautiful home in a great community, and it was worth the effort.

After about five years of commuting, I had moved up the ranks at work and completed my master's degree in criminal justice. I decided to take on a new role as an adjunct professor at the College of New Rochelle in the Bronx, my alma mater. While being an adjunct at the college, I got a call at my job from a familiar crew member's voice, informing me that their niece was in my class. He said he knew it was me because of how hyped up his niece was when telling him about the class. That was a full circle moment for me, the pregnant teenage girl whom he watched grow up, is now a college professor. Go figure.   Around the same time, I was promoted to forensic executive director at FEGS. As new career opportunities came our way, David and I never hesitated to cheer each other on. Around this time, David applied and obtained a promotion to a position as an Outreach Counselor in the Homeless Services unit at the Health Center. Shortly after, he became a state-certified HIV/AIDS counselor.

I was so proud of him. David had a skill set that went far beyond what the Health Center utilized. I saw it as a steppingstone to something greater—something more challenging and rewarding. But no matter how many conversations we had about him moving on, that was one area where my influence didn't work.

What I didn't realize was that David saw his work at the Health Center as a way of giving back to a community he had once contributed to harming. He loved seeing friends, family, and their children come in for services. He was responsible for homeless outreach in Mount Vernon, and he knew everyone. After all, he was Goose Seward, the unofficial mayor of Mount Vernon.

The Seward family was one of the largest in Mount Vernon, and they seemed to know everyone. I remember when I first met his mother and sisters, it felt like they were always coming from or going to a funeral. I thought it was strange. Who knows how many people have passed away?

One day, I asked David if his family attended funerals, whether they knew the person or not. He laughed and said, "No, we've been in this community for over 60 years. There are very few people we don't know. Every funeral we attend is for someone who's either a family member, a neighbor, an old schoolmate, or a friend of a friend." I was not convinced until years later, that's when I realized everyone in Mt. Vernon knew at least one Seward.

Meanwhile, my career path had taken me into academia and leadership. After applying for a position within the FEGS forensic case management program, I was hired as assistant director, and less than a year later, the director, Pat, resigned to become assistant commissioner of the NYC

Department of Mental Health and Hygiene. I then became director. Under my leadership, several FEGS case managers had the opportunity to visit prisons and see firsthand where most of our clients came from. For many, it was eye-opening. For me, it was the most fulfilling part of my career. I felt like I was keeping my word to return in a better position to bring about real change.

The change I brought was rooted in connection: making community-based programs available to those inside and ensuring that people on the outside understood the needs of those returning home. I wasn't just visiting—I was building bridges.

Going in and out of state prisons, I met so many people—correctional executives, counseling staff, and incarcerated individuals. What I didn't realize at first was that every year, people inside looked forward to seeing my team and me at the resource fairs. Before long, other state and even federal facilities reached out, asking me to attend their events. That's when I truly understood the importance of prison in-reach—not just for those incarcerated, but also for the correctional counseling staff. Many correctional staff from various levels of government didn't attend community-based events and lacked the networks and resources that could help their clients succeed after release.

Beyond the prison walls, I developed programs for state agencies and supervised both city, state, and federal-funded initiatives providing mental health services to people coming home from jail and prison with documented severe mental health diagnoses. My knowledge of the criminal justice system, combined with my academic credentials, opened doors. I was invited to meetings with government officials at every level. It was humbling and thrilling to be one of the few people I knew from school who was actually working in their field of study.

I was also a good manager. That was not just my opinion; my staff and the FEGS Human Resource director also shared my sentiment. The staff gave me accolades and thoughtful gifts during the holidays. Many still say I was the best supervisor they ever had—even those I had to let go. Most were in entry-level case management roles, and I took it upon myself to be more than a boss. I was a mentor. For some, I was like a mother. It might have been unorthodox, but we functioned like a family, and we got the work done.

I always encouraged my staff to grow. Whether applying for a new position within the agency, stepping into something different, or pursuing a degree, I pushed them to chase their goals or to develop some.

One day, a staff member came into my office with a job announcement. It was for the Executive Director position at the Brooklyn District Attorney's ComALERT program—the first full-service reentry program in the country run out of a prosecutor's office. She said, "I think you'd be a good fit for this job. You should apply."

I looked at her and said, "Are you trying to get rid of me?"

She laughed and replied, "Of course not. I just want to see you grow."

Because I had always preached growth and opportunity, I could not ignore her encouragement. So, I applied.

And I got the job.

I was offered the position of Executive Director of ComALERT at the Kings County (Brooklyn) District Attorney's Office under DA Charles Hynes. When I told David, he looked at me like I had lost my mind. "You're going to work for the DA?" he asked. Then, in true David fashion, he said, "OK, Boo."

Although I was ecstatic, it was another bittersweet moment in my career. I was leaving a team I had built, a community I had served, and clients I had grown to care deeply about. But I knew this was the next step in my journey, and I was ready. If I did not say Thank You to Lila G., let the record reflect eighteen years later, I am saying thank you. The seed you watered has grown beyond belief.

I was teaching college two nights a week and running a forensic program that served people coming out of city, state, and federal prisons. I led a case management team of about 15 staff members who worked with individuals returning home from incarceration with severe mental illness, many of whom were also unhoused.

The work was intense but deeply fulfilling. I met people at every level of the criminal justice system. During this time, I began sending my team into prisons to participate in resource fairs and speak at events hosted by organizations run by the people who lived there.

The morning of my first day at the Brooklyn District Attorney's Office, as I prepared for work and fought off nerves, David reminded me, "Brooklyn is a horse of another color." He remembered Brooklyn from the 1960s and 1970s, describing it as the Wild West. I arrived knowing very little about the County of Kings (Brooklyn) and anxious about how a prosecutor's office could truly support people coming home from prison.

I walked in bracing for bureaucratic nonsense—and found the opposite.

Although it later became known that there were questionable practices in the Brooklyn DA's Office under District Attorney Charles Hynes, I have to say this: when it came to reentry programming, he was serious. I often tell people who question my time there that I was not involved in prosecution—I was focused on services and programs for people returning home from prison. Whether his motivation was conscience or calculation, I can say with certainty that he was committed to the cause. He constantly looked for innovative ways to educate his staff and engage the Brooklyn community, especially the faith-based community, about people coming home from prison. As a result, Brooklyn became a hub for community-based services that welcomed justice-involved individuals at every level.

About 30 days into my role as Executive Director of ComALERT, I received a visit from Dr. Divine Pryor, then one of the Executives of Nu Leadership on Urban Solutions, a nonprofit think tank comprised of formerly incarcerated people. Nu Leadership challenged conventional thinking about crime and punishment, bringing together lived experience, collective accountability, and policy expertise. It was our first time meeting. He told me he had been sent to "check me out" and make sure I was the right fit. I never questioned who sent him; I just engaged in the conversation. He also shared that Brooklyn had the highest number of people returning from prison and the highest number going in. Dr. Pryor shared with me the findings from the 2006 Million Dollar Block survey, which showed that in a few blocks in Brooklyn's Brownsville and East New York neighborhoods, the taxpayers were paying $1 million each year to incarcerate residents. Which was shocking to me, but it provided some insight into the task ahead of me. We talked for hours. Before he left, he gave me his seal of approval. To this day, he remains a confidant, mentor, brother, and friend.

After that meeting, word spread quickly: the sister running ComALERT was about her business and here to help people coming home from prison.

One of my responsibilities at the DA's Office was to bring faith- and community-based organizations to the table, ensuring they were ready to support returning citizens. Somehow, I became a spokesperson for prisoner reentry. Invitations started coming from across the country—Atlanta, Chicago, Los Angeles, New Jersey, Philadelphia—

and from the city, state, and federal prison and jail systems. Even though I knew I was knowledgeable, I still second-guessed myself at times.

I often sat at the table with New York State Secretary of State Denise O'Donnell, helping develop reentry strategies and state programs. One of the programs I helped design—the New York State County Reentry Task Force—is still operating today, with some modifications. That is something I am incredibly proud of.

Throughout all of this, David was right by my side. He was never intimidated by my success. He supported me, celebrated me, and was proud of everything I accomplished. While I was busy with criminal justice events, we would choose which events he would attend. Never any pressure from me. He did not care for panel discussions; he would say most of the people on stage did not know what they were talking about and were just quoting textbooks. David also believed that, after some time out of prison, a person should not feel obligated to keep declaring they were formerly incarcerated—because, hopefully, by then, they had made great progress and should not be defined by the lowest point of their lives. I understood his point, but I also knew the value of speaking about life's discomforts to help keep people focused and on track. Still, he never missed an award ceremony. He was always there, proud and smiling, when I was recognized for my work.

At the time, David was still working at the Mount Vernon Neighborhood Health Center and doing well. All the kids were grown and living life on their own terms. Both of our families were cheering me on as I rose in the field of criminal justice. David had already made peace with his past; going back to prison was no longer an option. He enjoyed spending time with his aging mother, being with family, and living life on life's terms. He went on guys' bus trips to Atlantic City or played poker on Fridays. We were living our lives and enjoying the balance between work, family, and fun.

Although my career was thriving, I found myself restless. About three months after completing my master's degree, I decided to pursue a PhD in Criminal Justice. Knowing my schedule could not allow for a traditional, in-person program, I enrolled in an online program at Capella University.

I did not know exactly what lay ahead—I just knew I missed the academic environment. I had grown so used to incorporating homework into my downtime that I barely remembered what I liked to do for fun. Watching TV or going to the movies felt like a treat. So, once again, I told David, "I'm going back to school." And, as always, he said, "OK, Boo."

By this time, David knew me well. He knew my brain moved a mile a minute and that I was always chasing something meaningful. He also knew I had professional goals that included bringing change to the criminal justice system. He never interfered with my growth—whether academic, mental, spiritual, or personal.

Completing the PhD coursework was the easy part. Writing the dissertation? That was the real challenge. There were times I felt like quitting. Thank God for my dissertation chairperson, Dr. Henderson. He was not just my PhD Chairperson —he was my therapist, too. He always reminded me, "If getting a PhD were easy, more people would have one." He also reminded me that Capella University does not support ABD—all but dissertation— as it does not hold the same status.

It took me about eight years to complete the program, including writing and defending my dissertation. In August 2012, I crossed the finish line. I became Dr. Vanda Seward.

David and I would laugh about it. I would say, "How are you going to handle people calling me Dr. Seward?" And he would reply, "If someone asks me if I'm Dr. Seward's husband, I'm going to say, 'Yes, I'm that ___ husband.'" And we would laugh together.

My graduation ceremony was held in Minnesota. Only my mother and David attended. During one of the events, I turned to my mom and said, "I know you're surprised to be here." She replied, "I'm not surprised." But I knew better.

My brother had always been the "hero child." He graduated from high school, went straight to college, and was married when his children were born. I was the teenage mother, the high school dropout, the one who married someone incarcerated. I was not supposed to surpass him academically—but I did.

The proud moment of earning my doctorate was a culmination of years of relentless dedication, a testament to the belief that one's past does not dictate one's future. David's unwavering support was, as always, the bedrock upon which my achievements were built. He had seen me through every late-night study session, every stressful exam, and every moment of self-doubt, and his quiet strength never faltered. Now, with "Dr. Vanda Seward" firmly affixed to my name, a new chapter was unfolding—one that promised even greater opportunities to enact the change I was so passionate about. The desire to push boundaries and make a tangible impact within the criminal justice system had never waned.

After my graduation, the momentum continued. The world of reentry programming and advocacy felt like my true calling, and the doors that had opened were leading me to increasingly influential positions. My work at the Brooklyn DA's Office, though under the shadow of broader controversies, had solidified my commitment to providing tangible support for those reentering society. The connections forged, the programs designed, and the lives touched had left an indelible mark. I found myself speaking at conferences more frequently, mentoring younger professionals, and continuing to build bridges between correctional facilities and community-based organizations. David, ever the steady presence, would still accompany me to some events, his quiet pride a constant reassurance. He'd often joke about the "Dr." title, but beneath the humor was a deep respect for the journey I had undertaken.

Yet even with the academic triumph and career advancement, a familiar restlessness began to stir. The educational environment, the constant pursuit of knowledge, and the intellectual challenges were a magnetic force. David knew this inherent drive in me. He understood that my mind was perpetually engaged, seeking out the next meaningful endeavor. He had witnessed my passion for transforming the criminal justice system, and he never once tried to hold me back. The thought of further exploration—of delving deeper into the nuances of criminal justice policy and practice—began to take root, a whisper of a new academic pursuit, a potential return to the structured world of learning that had so often propelled me forward.

The years that followed my PhD were a whirlwind of professional growth and personal fulfillment. While Dr. Vanda Seward was now a recognized title, I remained Vanda to David—his "Boo," and the steady bedrock of our shared life. We continued our cherished 90-day getaways, though the destinations shifted from the familiar shores of San Juan to more ambitious explorations. We cruised through the Eastern and Western Caribbean, marveled at vibrant cultures, and even ventured where my fascination with local correctional facilities led us, at times, on some unexpected detours. David, ever the trooper, would patiently wait outside, with a smile on his face, while I indulged my unique curiosity, always returning with tales that—much to his amusement—didn't involve him in any jail cells.

My career trajectory continued to ascend. I transitioned from the DA's Office, embracing opportunities to impact policy and practice in criminal justice reform directly. I was invited to speak at national conferences, my voice amplified by lived experience and academic rigor. I found immense satisfaction in building bridges between communities and correctional institutions, creating programs that offered genuine support and a path toward rehabilitation. My team at the DA office and FEGS flourished under my leadership, and the mentorship I provided—much like the support David always offered me—became a hallmark of my professional life. David & I were a testament to the idea that success isn't a zero-sum game; our individual achievements only amplified our shared joy.

David, meanwhile, continued to thrive in his role at the Health Center, his compassion and dedication evident to everyone he encountered. He was Goose Seward, the unofficial mayor of Mount Vernon, a man who had found profound purpose in giving back to the community that had once been his struggle. He found contentment in the simple pleasures: family gatherings, quiet evenings, and the occasional bus trip to Atlantic City. Our lives were a tapestry woven with ambition and contentment—a balance of chasing dreams and savoring the moments, always with the quiet, unwavering strength of our love as the central thread.

Chapter 11
Breaking Barriers from Brooklyn to Albany

Knocking on Doors and Taking Names

"In government, they teach you that titles matter most. But I learned that relationships are everything—and no position can replace the trust you build one person at a time.

I thought I was joining a system (Parole) that wanted to change. Instead, I found myself fighting a system that was more interested in protecting itself than serving the communities it claimed to care about."

Two years into my role at the Brooklyn DA's Office—while also working on special projects with the New York State Division of Parole—I was presented with what I considered the opportunity of a lifetime. I applied for the position of Chairperson of the New York State Division of Parole. I was told that around 60 people applied. I'm not sure how many were interviewed, but I advanced to the final round, where it came down to just me and one other candidate—someone I knew and respected.

Ultimately, the position went to Andrea Evans, who had worked her way up through the ranks. At the time of her appointment, it was said that promoting an internal candidate would help boost morale within the parole division. I thought she was the right choice. I had partnered with her on several reentry projects while at the DA's Office and believed she could bring meaningful change.

Although I was not chosen as Chairperson, I was offered—and accepted—an appointment from then–Governor David Paterson to serve as Statewide Director of Reentry Services. In this role, I joined the executive cabinet of the New York State Division of Parole, where I worked alongside Evans to shape statewide reentry policy. Knowing who would be taking the chairperson position gave me confidence that real change was possible, since both of us understood the division's needs as a whole—its staff and the people under supervision.

It was another bittersweet moment. The team at ComALERT was dynamic—a mix of formerly incarcerated individuals and dedicated professionals—and we were doing groundbreaking work in Kings County. Leaving them behind, not knowing exactly what I was stepping into, was difficult. But when I spoke to DA Charles Hynes, he, without hesitation, said, "You are going to take that position. Not only can you do the job, but it also makes my office look good. You have nothing to worry about. If you are not satisfied, you can always return." My immediate supervisor, Lance Ogiste, was just as supportive. After hearing both of them say, "You can do it. You can handle it," I knew I had to take that leap of faith.

By then, although I admired the Serenity Prayer, I found myself living by Angela Davis's words: "I am no longer accepting the things I cannot change. I am changing the things I cannot accept."

Taking on the role of Statewide Director was not just a professional leap—it was a true test of my marriage. The first challenge was logistical: I had to maintain a residence in Albany. The second was emotional: on a good week, I was only home from Thursday night to Sunday afternoon.

There is something remarkable about the strength of a marriage when two people can live apart most of the time and still feel supported. David never wavered. I remember him coming with me to see the Albany apartment before I moved in, just to make sure everything was right.

As we drove to Albany, he said, "The only time I've ever traveled on Interstate 87 North was when I was going to prison." His words sat heavy in the car, carrying years of memory in a single sentence.

Along the way, he remembered his time working for Corcraft while in the industrial training program at Mt. McGregor Correctional Facility—delivering furniture from prison industries—and even brought up a Buffalo wing spot called Hurley's, a bar that had long since closed. I remembered it too; it was one of my stops on the long drives home after visiting him in prison.

But this time, he wasn't shackled to a bus, and I wasn't on my way to see him behind bars. He was sitting in the car beside me. That ride to Albany wasn't about prison anymore—it was about possibility.

And so began our five-year journey.

Working for the Division of Parole was an experience like no other. Across the state, upstate and down, some communities did not like or respect parole. The further north you went, the stronger the bias—racial and regional alike. Many upstate staff had little fondness for people from New York City. So, when both the Chairwoman and the Statewide Director of Reentry—two African American women from New York City—stepped into leadership, it was a nightmare for some staff north of the Tappan Zee Bridge.

At the time, state and federal funding for reentry services was pouring in. Agencies were encouraged—and sometimes pressured—to apply for public safety grants to support people returning home from prison. I was already deeply involved in statewide reentry strategy, often sitting at the table with commissioners, police chiefs, the governor's staff, and community leaders. Many claimed to support reentry, but too frequently those meetings felt like political posturing rather than real progress.

One meeting stands out. The DMV Commissioner proudly touted a policy to provide non-driver IDs to people leaving prison. But local offices were not following through. Despite repeated reports, he clung to the policy on paper until I kept pointing out the reality: people were being turned away. After months, he finally realized he was one of the few who even knew the policy existed. It was a wake-up call that policy without implementation is just noise. And there was always plenty of noise in those meetings.

Corrections would circulate quarterly reports boasting about IDs issued, shelter avoidance, and "Phase Three" reentry program completions. But with over 20 years of experience, I saw the flaws. Transfers, waitlists, and shallow programming left many unprepared. Public safety was at risk, while taxpayers' money funded everything but safety.

Those meetings were often tedious—I called them "the meeting before the meeting" because little ever got done. Secretary of State Denise O'Donnell had a visionary team, but even when agencies agreed to her initiatives, they went back to their offices and continued as usual.

Parole's biggest fear was bad press—someone under supervision committing a high-profile crime. So, they clung to a custody model, focusing on those labeled "high risk." Ironically, those who needed the most help often received the least.

COMPAS is an assessment tool that predicts reoffending risk using behavior and psychology-based questions, meant to assess needs and set supervision levels. Parole staff pushed back: "We've been doing this for 80 years. We don't need a tool." What they missed was that many weren't doing the job well, especially for those whose needs fell outside the extremes.

Some parole staff volunteered as trainers for career advancement. In contrast, others on the prison side sabotaged the process by letting incarcerated people fill out the tool themselves without guidance or direction. Parole officers often requested waivers before even meeting someone if they disagreed with the results. Sometimes the request was valid. Other times, it was pure bias.

By 2009, reentry programs were everywhere, but implementation was uneven. At a regional meeting in Western New York, one officer asked, "What do I do with someone who won't stop using drugs, now that we're told not to lock them up?" Clearly, staff had not been trained or supported in community-based alternatives. The old model—violate and incarcerate—was no longer acceptable, and many parole officers were lost in the process.

Eventually, I realized the dysfunction wasn't just at the ground level—it was systemic. Management operated on a "cover your ass" mentality. Mistakes were buried, blame was shuffled, and accountability depended on personal connections. The unspoken motto? "You're only as good as your last deed."

Yet along the way, I met extraordinary people—some formerly incarcerated, some not. One was Donna H., whom I first met at a Harlem reentry symposium. Months later, she called my office asking for a travel pass. At first, I thought she meant booking travel arrangements. Then she explained it was approval she needed from her parole officer so she could travel for work. I was stunned; I had no idea she was on parole. But that revelation never changed how I saw her—professional, sincere, and deeply committed. In fact, many advocates with justice involvement proved more grounded and authentic than some of the so-called professionals at the policy table.

At another symposium, I met Kathy B., after many had urged us to connect. It felt long overdue. The most meaningful relationships in my career often grew from prison work—relationships that thrived long after the prison gates closed.

I walked into facilities from Fishkill to Bedford Hills, Otisville to Sullivan, Orange to Taconic—sometimes with FEGS, sometimes with ComALERT, and later with Parole. Along the way, I met incredible people: C. Wilkins, Y. Johnson-Peterkin, V. Pate, G. Martin, M. DeVeaux, L. Rudolph, R. Simmons, Odell, K. Jones, J. Clarke, J. Robinson, E. Waters, J. Perez, R. Day, A. Dickson, V. Nixon, R. Smith, and so many others.

Today, many of those I met during or after incarceration are more than acquaintances—they are friends. In some cases, those friendships are stronger and more genuine than with people I've known for years who were never incarcerated.

People I engaged with from different walks of life and across many agencies often told me I was "real." At first, I wasn't sure what they meant. Over time, I understood that being part of a justice agency would never change who I was. Real was part of my DNA, woven into the fabric of my being—and it was the reason I could connect with some officials in Albany and many families across the state without losing myself.

I remember one Friday at the Albany Parole Central Office when Chairwoman Evans called me about a man named Mr. Rudolph at Queensboro. After nearly 30 years in prison, he refused release because DOCCS planned to send him to a New York City shelter—even though he was from Long Island. He told the corrections counselor, "Call her. I'm not leaving until she comes." That "her" was me.

I hadn't seen him in about six years, but he had followed my journey. When I walked into Queensboro Correctional Facility that Monday morning, he grinned at the counselor and said, "I told you she was coming." I laughed and asked him, "What the hell are you doing?" He smiled and shook his head. "After all the reentry programs I completed upstate, now they want to send me to a New York City shelter. I'm from Long Island. That's a setup for failure."

He was right. Then—and still now—DOCCS should not send people who served long sentences to shelters. New York City's homeless system has said repeatedly that it cannot provide the specialized support they need. Fortunately, Parole had contracted beds with a community-based organization at the time. I secured supportive housing in the Bronx, and his Osborne Association counselor managed the rest. Today, he is part of the aging population, living crime-free and contributing to his community.

Then there was K. Jones, whom I met at Fishkill Correctional Facility. He had gone to prison as a teenager and earned his BA while incarcerated. Because of his academic excellence, he was awarded a scholarship from Lincoln University in Pennsylvania to pursue a master's degree upon release. The challenge was that classes were held every Saturday in Philadelphia. He called me to ask if I could help him get permission to travel from his parole officer.

I reached out to one of the more community-minded Regional Directors, G. Walthall, and she agreed he would receive a weekend travel pass, contingent upon passing his classes. Like clockwork, he emailed me his transcripts each semester. He earned his master's and went on to complete his PhD.

While working at the Brooklyn District Attorney's Office, I often received calls from people on parole in Brooklyn with warrants for failure to report or for absconding, asking me for help turning themselves in. Word spread quickly. Before long, individuals even began coming directly to my office to surrender. I coordinated with Regional Director M. Smith and parole staff to make sure the process was safe and respectful.

Many came with loved ones—spouses and children—for strength. I helped families understand the process and tried to ease the emotional toll. For parole staff, these surrenders also carried less risk: entering the building on Joralemon Street meant passing through metal detectors, which added a layer of security.

I was fortunate at that time to work with Regional Director M. Smith, an excellent leader who knew her role well and carried a deep sense of humanity—regardless of whom she engaged with or the nature of their crime.

There are countless stories like these—moments when I could bring clarity, fairness, and humanity to a system that so often lacks all three. Whether working for DOCCS or the DA's Office, I made myself available to answer questions and troubleshoot concerns—not just for colleagues, but for families and anyone touched by these systems.

My colleagues and comrades spanned across small and large agencies across New York City and beyond: The Fortune Society, Osborne Association, RAPP, Alliance of Families for Justice, Exodus Transitional Services, Nu Leadership on Urban Solutions, Correctional Association, NYC Department of Health, NYC Department of Mental Health, NYS Psychiatric Center, Mustard Seed, National Action Network, Vertex, College and Community Fellowship, Green Hope, Alpha School, Bowery Residence Committee, Brightpoint, Buffalo Urban League, Saving Grace Ministries, NYC Commission on Human Rights—and many more. Just as I called them for help, they called on me. I always took my role seriously because I worked on their behalf. I made it my business to reassure them: you have a friend in government who won't compromise her integrity.

The relationships I built over 33+ years—with government and non-government entities, and with people impacted by the justice system—still exist today. Relationships are the backbone of this work. Whether with community-based organizations, other government agencies, or directly with justice-impacted people, those connections made progress possible. Many of the people I met early in my career have traveled with me for decades. In every role I've held—government, nonprofits, academia — it's those relationships that grounded me and reminded me who I was doing the work for. That is what I call real recognizing real.

I cannot recall every name of the good NYSDOCCS staff, but many deserve recognition. Some are retired, while others remain on the frontlines and behind the scenes, committed to doing their work with integrity and humanity for people in custody or under community supervision. I appreciated and respected their dedication.

The NYS DOCCS Reentry Services Unit (RESU)—staff like S. Dorsey (retired), D. Howell, M. Washington (retired), the late R. Baultwright, R. Mitchell (retired), D. McKoy (retired), A. Thompson, L. Connelly (retired), J. Reeves, and A. Enright (retired). — The RESU teams were across the state, located in the seven regional parole offices, which supervise individuals released from prison in the 63 counties that comprise the state of New York. Under my leadership, the RESU team was so dynamic that people within the department and communities still talk about their work. We not only developed programs but also held them accountable when they failed to serve people under supervision, while ensuring parole staff had the resources they needed. These colleagues were strong representatives of parole, and the community knew they did their work well.

Much of what RESU accomplished was made possible by dynamic Regional Directors and central office staff. M. Osborne and the Regional Directors in Western New York (Buffalo) and downstate (NYC)—Young, Smith, Russi, Walthall, Brown, and Townsend, all now retired—were essential to the success of the Reentry Services Unit. Together, we built a team that believed in accountability, fairness, and second chances. The weight of systemic dysfunction was a heavy cloak, but beneath it, the threads of genuine connection and impactful action were undeniable.

My five years as Statewide Director of Reentry Services were a testament to this duality. It was a constant push-and-pull between the entrenched bureaucracy, the fear of headlines, and the passionate advocacy of those on the ground, both inside and outside the system. I learned that true progress wasn't about grand announcements or policies, but about the quiet persistence of individuals like Mr. Rudolph and K. Jones, and about the unwavering support of my colleagues who saw people on parole, not just state numbers. In those moments—when a breakthrough was achieved, when a life was steered toward possibility—the exhaustion of endless meetings and frustrating roadblocks melted away.

The "cover your ass" mentality, while pervasive, was not the whole story. The dedicated staff within DOCCS and the Division of Parole—those who quietly went the extra mile—were the true bedrock. The RESU team, under my leadership, became a force precisely because we balanced accountability with unwavering support for the individuals we served. We didn't just develop programs; we ensured they were implemented with integrity, and that parole officers had the resources to do their jobs effectively—not just to enforce compliance, but to foster genuine rehabilitation. The Regional Directors, those unsung heroes scattered across the state, were instrumental in translating our vision into tangible action, bridging the gap between Albany's pronouncements and the realities faced by people returning to their communities.

My role became less about climbing the ladder and more about building bridges. The partnerships I cultivated—from the Fortune Society to the NYC Commission on Human Rights—were the engine of change: relationships built on shared purpose and mutual respect. When people touched by the justice system—or the professionals serving them—saw that I operated with integrity and genuine care, doors opened, and possibilities materialized. This work was never about titles; it was about the impact of human connection and unwavering advocacy.

The dysfunction inside the Division of Parole wasn't easily untangled. Despite new funding and bold promises, inertia and a "cover your ass" mindset too often replaced accountability. Even so, David's steady support of me and the dedication of colleagues and community advocates fueled me to keep closing the gap between policy and practice.

Stories like Mr. Rudolph's and K. Jones's were my compass. His refusal to accept a shelter placement that would set him up to fail—and the supportive housing we secured—proved that tailored help changes outcomes. Jones's weekend travel pass to attend graduate classes in Philadelphia—and his master's, then PhD—showed what's possible when the system chooses to champion potential. Those are the moments when real recognition turns a phrase into practice—and when change becomes real, too.

Angel Flight – All Hands on Deck

While working for the New York State Department of Corrections and Community Supervision (NYSDOCCS), I was contacted about a parolee who had relocated to

Washington State to live with his son. Tragically, his son passed away, and the parolee was soon hospitalized with a chronic illness. While applying for Medicaid in Washington, it was discovered that his name and Social Security information were inaccurate.

Washington State Parole reached out to the NY governor's office and then to New York State Parole, stating they could no longer keep him in Washington and that New York would need to arrange for his relocation. Chairwoman Evans informed me that this was a "hot case" because the request came through the governor's office. They were not optimistic about transporting him back to New York, as he was hospitalized and unable to travel independently. I was instructed to make every effort possible—and document everything.

I immediately contacted the Reentry Services Unit (RESU) team that was under my direction at the Manhattan Parole Office. Together, we began investigating what needed to be done and what bureaucratic hurdles we might face. We identified the parolee because one of his aliases matched his actual name. Another document in his file listed two Social Security numbers—the one Washington had was incorrect, but the other matched our records. That discovery allowed us to move forward.

I then negotiated with Washington to arrange an Angel Flight—a nonprofit organization that provides air transport for bedridden individuals, often at no or limited cost. To qualify, the medical facility had to complete specific paperwork, which they agreed to do. Within two weeks, Mr. Ruiz's paperwork was finalized, and he was flown back to New York via Angel flight to JFK Airport, heavily sedated.

Two reentry managers from the Reentry Services Unit in Queens—Mary and Denise—met the flight and arranged for an ambulance to transport Mr. Ruiz to Bellevue Hospital. When the ambulance arrived at Bellevue, staff from the Bronx and Manhattan RESU unit—Detrell, Stacey, and I— were already at Bellevue awaiting the transport. We orchestrated Mr. Ruiz's admission, which went smoothly because all his medical records traveled with him. With the hospital's social worker's help, we coordinated with the New York City Department of Homeless Services to place him at the Goldwater Nursing Facility.

The level of partnership involved in this case was extraordinary. One of the primary lessons I teach all my staff—no matter the agency—is that partnerships and relationships with community-based organizations and other government entities are key to success. Much of the work we do is not driven by policy or criteria, but by the relationships we build.

I've seen firsthand how relationships can move mountains. Mr. Ruiz's Angel Flight would not have happened without the dedication of the RESU team and trust between medical staff, parole officers, and nonprofit partners. It wasn't a policy that got him home. It was people.

This is why I've always made mentorship a cornerstone of my leadership. I don't just teach people how to do the work—I teach them how to be in the work. That means understanding boundaries, honoring relationships, and knowing when to step back so someone else can step forward.

The Mr. Ruiz case became a touchstone—a living testament to the power of connection. It wasn't just about transporting one-man home. It was about the years of credibility, collaboration, and compassion that made such a complex solution possible. The work was never about titles or authority; it was about ensuring the government's doors stayed open and that, when someone knocked, there was a real person on the other side ready to help.

This case reinforced what my entire career has taught me: relationships are the backbone of real change. The bonds formed inside prisons and in the community —between advocates and agency leaders, between elders and emerging professionals—are what make progress possible. And they are the reason that, more than 33 years later, many of the same people are still engaged in this work with me.

Back to Basics

Because of the nonsense many parole staff have endured, they learned how to "dance with the devil" and still get the work done. I respect them deeply, and I take my hat off to them. At DOCCS, your worth was measured by your last decision, never by your years of service, and in that system, the reality is that "shit rolls downhill." Too often, it is the parole officer at the bottom who bears the consequences, yet somehow, they keep showing up, carrying the weight of a system on their backs with little support, recognition, and even less reward.

The merger, though I call it a takeover, between the New York State Division of Parole and the Department of Correctional Services was a top-heavy plan that failed to adequately prepare Parole staff for what was to come. On paper, it was meant to streamline operations, eliminate duplication, improve outcomes, enhance public safety, and save taxpayer dollars. In reality, it did none of those things.

What it did, and still does, is waste taxpayer money. The only real change was creating a new civil service title that allowed correction officers to become parole officer trainees. Under this system, anyone with a four-year degree, regardless of the field, could supervise people returning from prison. That meant someone with a degree in business, accounting, or IT could suddenly be responsible for individuals with histories of substance use, mental health challenges, and long-standing trauma. No background in human services required. To me, that made one thing clear: rehabilitation was not DOCCS's priority.

Parole staff at all levels were nervous. They felt excluded from the process and uncertain about the future. Once the merger was finalized, especially at the executive level, many became intimidated. Years of experience in community supervision suddenly seemed irrelevant. Some resorted to "shucking and jiving" just to make it through the day and reach retirement.

When Chairwoman Evans was not reappointed, and Assistant Commissioner Jimenez was appointed as Deputy Commissioner of Community Supervision (Parole), and Chairwoman Evans was appointed Assistant Commissioner, a measure of safety and security remained in the way parole staff did their work—DC Jimenez, was familiar with parole practices and was not afraid to share her opinions with others in the NYS DOCCS executive cabinet. Yet whispers spread that she could not be trusted, that she might "throw the baby out with the bathwater." It was a reminder that in systems built on control, even those who work within parole can become each other's targets. I knew Jimenez before I came to parole. We worked together in the community on special projects. From my perspective, she was very knowledgeable about parole operations and was very personable. No complaints, no problems. I knew everyone in leadership positions, including me, came with some baggage, and some may not agree with this, but neither DC Jimenez nor I resorted to shucking and jiving. We wanted to bring change and make decisions that improved the conditions for parole staff and people under community supervision.

Eventually, DC Jimenez retired, and former Chairwoman Evans remained Assistant Commissioner. Under Jimenez, Evans seemed level-headed and composed. I thought I knew Evanswell. But once she reported to the new Deputy Commissioner, Thomas Herzog, everything changed. Like many others, she was visibly shaken.

DC Herzog had a long history in corrections. Most executives on the community supervision side feared him. They let him say and do whatever he pleased, rarely offering correction or insight. Too many were busy protecting their pensions or avoiding reassignment to the field. I understood that instinct to a degree, but at what point does a DOCCS staff member stop compromising their integrity, morals, and values just to keep a pension? Some may say worrying about your pension is a major concern. I agree, however, the lack of integrity and one's willingness to compromise one's sense of humanity did not occur overnight. It was a slow process, but you knew because in most cases your conscience told you the situation or your actions were not right. When you realize that you were selling your soul, morals, and values from the start, you should reposition yourself. This negative decision-making process does not happen overnight. It's ingrained in the culture of NYSDOCCS, and it sucks up the vulnerable and those eager to make it to the top by hook or by crook. The ethical choices many DOCCS staff had to weigh went far beyond anything taught in the academy or any classroom.

I did not grow up in the state system. I had some rebel in my blood. In addition, I knew from day one of accepting my appointment with parole that I could return to the Brooklyn District Attorney's office at any time. I wasn't worried about DC Herzog. I knew my job, and all I needed to understand was his vision for my department and for community supervision as a whole.

Shortly after his arrival, I was asked to prepare a report on the Reentry Services Unit for DC Herzog. I asked AC Evans if she had suggestions on format or tone. She told me, "Dazzle him." I replied, "I don't know anything about dazzling him, but I'll get him the report." I didn't ask what she meant—I knew I wasn't about to dazzle any white man who carried himself like a dictator. Frankly, she often seemed two seconds away from calling him Massa.

It soon became clear that Evans had a problem with the fact that I would not kneel to the almighty DC Herzog. I don't think he could grasp it either. I was not skipping around either of them. Me! skipping anywhere for any reason was not happening for many reasons.

After Senator Jeffrey Klein revealed in late 2013 that there were sex offenders currently housed in family shelters throughout New York City, parole was now dealing with a sex offender crisis. I vividly remember a meeting held to strategize the sex offender housing crisis in New York City. DC Herzog ordered that all individuals on supervision with sex offender designations be removed from a Bronx nursing home and placed in city shelters—even those in wheelchairs, and those with other serious medical conditions.

Months prior, I visited that Bronx nursing home and knew the residents there had chronic medical conditions. I immediately spoke up, explaining that moving them would be harmful and burdensome for parole staff because ambulette services would be required. I further noted that people who are not ambulatory cannot be processed in the NYC shelter system at the Department of Homeless Services intake unit at Bellevue Hospital. You could have heard a pin drop. AC Evans looked shocked that I spoke up. In my mind, she should have said something. She was from New York City—she knew who qualified for that nursing home. But when job security becomes the priority, integrity is too often pushed aside.

After the meeting, she pulled me aside and said I had misspoken and needed to find another placement. My response was "Uh-uh." But nothing ever came of it, the urgency dissolved, and the plan was quietly abandoned, like so many others.

There were many moments when AC Evans' character faltered. She knew I had earned my PhD in Criminal Justice. One day, she called me into her office and told me I should not sign memos as "Dr. Seward." When I asked why—pointing out that I worked in the criminal justice field and it was academically and professionally appropriate—she had no real answer. Instead, she gave an odd example: "If you sign in at a restaurant as Dr. Seward and someone has a medical emergency, they'll come looking for you." I replied, "Then I'll let them know I'm not a medical doctor." She had nothing more to say.

I was baffled. Later, I shared the exchange with my doctoral mentor. He told me, "Don't worry. You'll get that from people in executive positions who may only have a bachelor's degree." I hadn't checked her credentials before—but I did after that. He was right. She only had a four-year degree and had envy with no respect for the academic acculturation and grit it takes to earn a doctorate, although she appeared to be supportive.

Looking back, I don't think it was really about memos or titles. It was about trying to shake my stability, because she thought I was too grounded, too confident in what I brought to the table, and too sure of who I was. Unfortunately, at 5 feet 9 and over 200 pounds, shaking me up does not come easily. Besides, I'm a Bronx girl; resilience was stitched into my DNA long before I earned any title.

I gathered that because she could not break me, she decided to get under my skin. What followed was a series of shenanigans initiated by her or dictated to her by Deputy Commissioner Herzog. In the winter of 2014, I was invited by a community-based organization to sit on a panel at the Black, Puerto Rican, Hispanic & Asian Legislators Caucus in Albany—a space I regularly attended and where I was well known. Following protocol, I informed AC Evans about the invitation, and she abruptly stated that she would be on the panel instead. She never consulted the organizers—she just decided.

I did not argue. I simply told the organizers she had replaced me. They were disappointed—not only because I would no longer be participating, but because she had inserted herself without notice. Two days before the event, she asked me to share my notes and talking points. What she did not know was that I never use notes. I speak from lived experience; it is all in my head. So, she was left to prepare her own remarks and PowerPoint.

What she also didn't realize was that projector access had to be requested in advance. On the day of the event, she was unable to show her slides. The organizers might have accommodated her, but that is what happens when you assume your title gives you free rein. Her presentation fell flat. Many in the audience were already angry about her past decisions as Chairwoman of the Parole Board. They had expected a change for the better in parole decisions under her leadership, and that had not happened. The frustration in the room was palpable. Had it not been for State Senator Ruth Hassell-Thompson interjecting, the audience—made up of community advocates and justice-impacted people—would have eaten her alive.

Following the panel, a light lunch was served. A special seating area was reserved for panelists. She was not invited to join the group, but my people had a seat waiting for me. By Monday, she was clearly upset. All that preparation, and still she did not get the reception she expected. That is what happens when you do not understand relationships and believe a title is everything.

By this time, the job's stress was taking its toll. I was suffering from migraines and erratic blood pressure. Yet the sex offender housing crisis in NYC continued. In response, some regional directors and executives decided to place reentry staff under the direct supervision of local regional management. It was another one of their "great idea" that backfired—limiting staff engagement with the community and undermining the very relationships they needed to do their jobs. You cannot build or maintain community-based resources from behind a desk. Today, RESU unit staff are still using this behind-the-desk approach to establish and maintain community ties, which is a model that does not build community capacity.

Reentry staff were on the phone daily, trying to secure housing for individuals with sex offense histories—often without success. Thanks to a lead from my longtime colleague, D. Lester from Queens parole RESU, and community partner, P. Henderson, I secured more than 50 SARA-compliant beds, 1000 feet from a school in Far Rockaway, NY. The Sexual Reform Act (SARA) places mandatory conditions on individuals convicted of certain sex crimes or on the state sex offender registry under community supervision (parole). Securing these beds at $35 per night was a deal that parole could not turn down. Immediately, parole began moving people into the shared housing. Unfortunately, shortly after the first meeting with the housing providers, I went on medical leave due to migraines and uncontrolled blood pressure—undoubtedly caused by the stress of the job.

What had once been a rewarding role became a daily battle. Each morning, I walked into the office wondering what AC Evans would do or say next. Her vendetta, in my view, stemmed from one thing: she could not break me. I would not bow to her—or to DC Herzog.

Even while on leave, I worked from home to maintain those 50 beds. But Parole always assumed they had the upper hand. A bureau chief in Queens parole office, whose people skills left much to be desired, nearly cost NYSDOCCS parole all the beds because of his mishandling and blatant disrespect to the housing provider. I got a call from a NYSDOCCS employee asking me to intervene behind the scenes because NYSDOCCS could not risk losing 50 beds for sex offenders. I made the call, resolved the issue, and shortly afterward, a regional director called to say, "I don't care what anyone says—I know you had something to do with getting those beds back. Thank you."

Not long after, I received an email from AC Evans directing me to report to the DOCCS Inspector General, while I was still on leave. My first thought was that she must have been angry that I was able to restore the beds when she could not. I refused to come in, which only upset her more; in her mind, anyone else would have complied without question.

When I asked what the meeting was about, I was told it concerned mileage sheets I had submitted for use of a state vehicle—basic entries listing mileage and destinations, not tied to any reimbursement. To me, it was nothing more than manufactured nonsense, another attempt to rattle me. And if that was the best they had, it only proved how desperate they were to break me. I never reported, and although I was not visibly worried, it was taking a toll on my health.

After six months under my doctor's care, and at the urging of my doctors, my husband, and those closest to me, I decided to resign from the New York State Department of Corrections and Community Supervision. It shocked many. People, as I have said previously, rarely resign from "a good state job." For those who had spent their careers within DOCCS, it was hard to imagine life beyond that system.

Sadly, once I left, the reentry unit's wings were clipped. Perhaps the RESU team had been too helpful—too committed to ensuring parole officers had the tools they needed to support people returning home from prison.

What most did not know was that I returned to the Brooklyn District Attorney's Office as one of the executives with the Kings County Reentry Task Force, under the direction of the New York State Division of Criminal Justice Services (NYSDCJS).

I recall attending the 2015 NYS Legislators Black and Puerto Rican Caucus and another event in Albany. DOCCS colleagues would greet me with, "Oh, I see you're doing well," or "Glad to see you got back on your feet." I wondered—when was I ever off my feet? But for those who only knew life inside DOCCS, it was impossible to envision anything beyond that paradigm.

I am not cut from that cloth. My experience, education, and knowledge of criminal justice extend far beyond DOCCS. That alone was enough for me to walk away from any job that threatened my health or my integrity.

A few years later, I applied for the position of Assistant Commissioner at the NYPD. During my background check, the investigator from the NYC Department of Investigation appeared uneasy before telling me what information he had received during a phone call from someone in the DOCCS executive office, who had given me a bad reference, claiming I had been "brought up on charges." Then, in the same breath, the source had said DOCCS would rehire me. The officer admitted it didn't make sense—he had never heard anything like it—but he had to record what he was told. In the end, I did not get the position. Because most of the community supervision office staff at the central office in Albany were new, I believe it was the NYSDOCCS executive director at that time who gave the fabricated information.

I was stunned. I knew my record was clean. The executive, I believe, fabricated my reference with the intent to discredit me, revealing far more about them than it did me. I filed a Freedom of Information request for my personnel file, determined to see for myself. When it came back, the truth was clear: there was nothing—no record of disciplinary action, no charges, nothing at all—just my application and benefits paperwork.

I immediately notified the DOCCS commissioner and the State Attorney General's office. I also filed a lawsuit, but it was dismissed because I missed the filing deadline by two days. That was fine with me—the executive team now knew I had filed, and that was enough. Later, when I called HR to get some information, the staffer told me, "I have your file on my desk. The same information you're asking about, I was looking for earlier. There is nothing but your application and benefit forms."

That moment confirmed something I already knew: I had shaken DOCCS enough that they wanted to smear my name. However, filing the lawsuit, even if unsuccessful, put them on notice. I was not afraid. I wasn't going to badmouth them or play their game. I was going to stand in my truth and demand mutual respect.

Parole staff who knew me—either before or during my time at DOCCS—understood the credibility and influence I brought to the table. One lesson I always stressed to reentry staff was that relationships are everything. Without them, this work cannot be done.

The aftermath of the lawsuit, even though dismissed, served as a quiet victory. It sent a message, loud and clear, that I wouldn't be silenced or smeared. My departure from DOCCS left a void, particularly in the Reentry Services Unit, a team I had poured my heart and soul into. We had built something significant, a dynamic force that had truly impacted the lives of individuals returning from incarceration. It was a testament to what could be achieved when integrity, compassion, and a deep understanding of people's needs were at the forefront. The fear that followed my resignation, the quiet clipping of the unit's wings, spoke volumes about the resistance to genuine progress within the system.

Even "off my feet," as some colleagues perceived it, my connection to the work and the people it served remained unshackled. The knowledge that my efforts had challenged the status quo enough to warrant such a retaliatory smear campaign was, in a strange way, validating. It reinforced my belief that standing in my truth, demanding mutual respect, and prioritizing integrity over a pension were the only paths worth taking. The resilience forged in the Bronx, and my unwavering belief in my own capabilities, were the armor that protected me from the corrosive conspiracies of a system that prioritized control over humanity.

The foundation of my career, the bedrock upon which I continued to build, was always relationships. Whether it was advocating for a parolee needing specialized housing, securing a master's degree for a scholar released from prison, or navigating the convoluted bureaucracy of state agencies, it was the human connections that made progress possible. These were the bridges I had built, the ones I would continue to cross and encourage others to traverse, knowing that in the complex landscape of justice reform, real change happened through relationships, not policy alone.

Throughout my career, one question I'm frequently asked is: "Should you share your contacts when you're leaving an organization?" It's a valid question, especially in fields like criminal justice, social work, and advocacy, where relationships often determine outcomes more than policies do.

My best practice is to provide general contact numbers—main office lines or publicly listed emails. Still, I do not share personal cell phone numbers or direct lines without prior approval. This isn't just about privacy; it's about respect. The relationships I've built over the years are rooted in trust, mutual understanding, and shared values. They are not transactional and certainly not transferable.

I always remind my staff and mentees that relationships must be earned. You can't inherit someone else's rapport with a community partner, legislator, or service provider. You have to show up consistently, listen deeply, and follow through. That's how trust is built, and that's how systems begin to shift.

The question of sharing contacts has always underscored a principle that guided my career: relationships are the currency of progress. To simply hand over a list of names would be to devalue the years of effort, empathy, and consistent engagement that went into building those connections. Genuine rapport isn't inherited; it's cultivated. It requires presence, patience, and proof. Policy may outline the work, but relationships are what make the work possible.

Back to Brooklyn

Coming back to the Kings County District Attorney's Office was a welcome relief, with many familiar faces. Working under the late DA Ken Thompson was a very different experience. He was a no-nonsense leader, and many seemed afraid to speak up around him, avoiding necessary conversations about programmatic needs. In my opinion, he placed people in executive roles who lacked a deep understanding of reentry as a whole and programming, and as a result, many key programs seemed watered down. When I arrived, the staff were already dissatisfied with the changes under the new administration.

Under the late DA Charles Hynes, programs had been a top priority. No matter what the forum, he always found a way to highlight his office initiatives, especially ComALERT, the first full-service reentry program in the country. Today, people may question his legacy—particularly in light of wrongful convictions—but when it came to reentry, he was ahead of his time.

I cannot speak to what took place in the trial divisions. Still, I can say the programs like ComALERT, Project Redirect, and domestic violence initiatives under DA Hynes were visibly and consistently supported. That commitment made a real impact on the programs.

When I returned to the Brooklyn DA's Office, I was struck by how much had changed. ComALERT and the County Reentry Task Force operated as two separate programs under one umbrella. ComALERT's once-renowned name—known across Brooklyn and the nation—had faded. In the push to create a new program for the new DA to "hang his hat on," the name Charles Hynes was quietly removed, and with it, the program's identity and visibility.

People would often ask, "What happened to ComALERT?" I would respond, "Nothing—it still exists." But the follow-up was always the same: "Well, we haven't seen or heard anything about it." The truth was, ComALERT had become a shadow of its former self. It had once been a national model. When I first became Executive Director in 2007, dignitaries from around the world visited to learn from our approach. District attorneys from other states came to replicate the model. Now, it felt like a relic.

The County Reentry Task Force had also shifted. Reporting criteria limited eligibility to individuals within 45 days of release. That is not nearly enough time for someone with complex needs. It can take more than 45 days just to secure public assistance, obtain a state ID, start treatment, or find stable housing. The change was designed to show data reflecting "satisfactory participation," but research shows it takes at least 90 days for someone to begin stabilizing.

Building relationships between parole staff and the DA's office was another challenge. I had strong connections, but the model seemed more focused on numbers than services. The reentry staff who had been there before 2009 had lost their spark. Everything now felt like an obstacle.

There was a time when the DA's reentry program was a household name in Brooklyn. During my tenure as Executive Director, ComALERT staff were everywhere— doing prison in-reach, joining block parties, attending resource fairs, and supporting people coming home with their families. That energy was missing.

To be fair, I do not personally blame the late DA Ken Thompson. The lack of support came from his executive team, which failed to emphasize the importance of reentry work. Still, I maneuvered through the noise and kept moving forward.

Under my leadership, we launched the Community Report Initiative with the Brooklyn Community Supervision (parole)Office. Instead of waiting hours at a parole office, individuals could meet their parole officers at the DA's task force office on Joralemon Street. These visits included a one-hour information session featuring presentations on psychoeducation, job development, and empowerment groups—led by guest speakers, parole staff, or DA staff. It was a win-win: parole officers had a less stressful work environment, and clients received meaningful engagement.

With Mighty Shero Productions, playwrights, and DA staff, we produced an original play, Here to Be Seen: Women and Justice, highlighting the challenges women face before, during, and after incarceration. Over 300 people attended the one-night performance at Poly Tech University. The evening began with light refreshments and a violist who played R&B and jazz, setting a warm, vibrant tone. Many attendees later said it felt like a night on Broadway, a powerful mix of art, justice, and community.

I also organized the first sex offender training at the Brooklyn DA's office for professional staff and community members. The administration expected little interest, but the room was packed—standing room only. People are always eager to learn about this issue. The new administration seemed unaware, or the old had forgotten, that I had a long history of organizing impactful conferences and workshops.

Mighty Shero Productions and I also staged a rendition of The Vagina Monologues, about women's experiences with sex, love, tenderness, pain, and resilience. The cast included actresses from Orange Is the New Black, formerly incarcerated women, and me. We performed at Taconic, Edgecombe, and Queensboro state prisons, Fortune Society, and finally at the Cherry Lane Theatre in New York City, where I made my off-Broadway debut. It was unforgettable. The audience was deeply moved by the raw truth of the monologues and the powerful presence of the cast—women from diverse walks of life united by shared purpose.

While struggling with a debilitating knee issue and having to wait over three years for insurance approval for knee replacement surgery, and feeling that my role at the Brooklyn DA's Office was no longer fulfilling, I chose to retire. While still weighing the decision, a new opportunity appeared—one I knew was divine alignment. I was offered a tenure-track Assistant Professor position in the Criminal Justice Department at City University of New York, Kingsborough Community College.

This was God's work. My purpose in pursuing a PhD had always been to retire early and transition into academia. So, there was no hesitation. The theme of my retirement party was Passing the Torch. Too often, we forget to prepare the next generation of professionals. Whether you wanted to be a lawyer, correctional officer, police officer, or policymaker, academia was where I could do my part.

What I have learned since is that there is a real need for practitioners in academic spaces. Criminal justice cannot be fully understood from textbooks alone. Lived experience, practical knowledge, and community engagement are essential to teaching it well.

One of the most rewarding parts of Kingsborough is staying connected to the community while bringing criminal justice forums directly to campus. This role has broadened my perspective and reaffirmed that criminal justice education is more than coursework—it is context, culture, and connection.

Within the first months, I launched the college's first criminal justice radio show: Vision and Solutions: Criminal Justice Evolution. The weekly hour-long program featured community leaders, scholars, grassroots organizers, and others discussing policy, reform, and lived experiences. It was lively, informative, and accessible—reaching listeners on iTunes and Spotify. Unfortunately, COVID put the show on hold, but for the two and a half years I hosted and edited it, it was incredibly rewarding. It brought criminal justice issues to the forefront in ways that were both educational and empowering.

Now, nearly four years into my role at CUNY Kingsborough, I was offered the position of Director of the Criminal Justice Program. It was a full-circle moment—one filled with both pride and reflection. The offer felt like a testament to years of hard-won battles and unwavering dedication, the culmination of a journey marked by both the exhilaration of progress and the sting of systemic resistance. Even as I stepped into this new chapter, the echoes of my departure from DOCCS remained—a reminder of the smear attempts that never succeeded but revealed the lengths to which some will go to maintain power. I carried that lesson with me: resilience is not just about enduring, but about refusing to be shaped by the smallness of others.

This was the transition I had envisioned when I pursued my PhD—a move into academia where I could prepare the next generation of justice practitioners. My retirement celebration was themed "Passing the Torch," a clear acknowledgment that the work must continue beyond any one person. Teaching gave me the space to merge theory with lived experience, bringing context, community, and accountability into the classroom.

Chapter 12
The Advocate

An Unshakable Alliance

"Advocacy means refusing to stay silent, even when silence would be easier. It means standing where others fall away."

Before I entered the gates of Edgecombe Correctional Facility in 1986, my understanding of prison was limited to visiting a childhood friend. I loved The Escorts' album—"All We Need Is Another Chance" (1973). I loved the prison pictures taken of them recording music while incarcerated, and I knew a few people from the streets who had cycled in and out of prison. I visited the Bronx House of Detention on River Avenue and Rikers Island a few times, though those memories are foggy.

When I arrived at Edgecombe, I was struck by the constant movement—men transferring from upstate prisons into work release. Some came prepared for the transition from prison to the community, but many did not. They were eager to work, reunite with their families, and begin again, but few had concrete plans. Employment was one of the greatest barriers. At the time, it was still legal for employers to reject applicants solely for having a criminal record. Family reunification was often just as difficult.

Many returned home to families still grappling with addiction or mental health struggles. Others relapsed—addictions suppressed in prison resurfaced once they were back in the community. These setbacks undermined work-release goals and fueled recidivism. Unlike today, data on recidivism in the 1980s weren't widely collected or studied. It wasn't until the 1980s that the Bureau of Justice Statistics started collecting data on arrests, but in 2005, it enhanced the data collection to include recidivism data that was open to the public. In 2001, New York's Department of Correctional Services began examining recidivism trends, including the impact of earning a GED while incarcerated. But I didn't need a study to know what I was already witnessing: the system was failing people.

These experiences pushed me toward advocacy. I saw the urgent need for stronger in-prison programming and more robust community-based reentry services. Over the years, my advocacy has taken many forms. I've been called upon by government and nonprofit organizations to weigh in on legislative bills, contribute to grant-writing strategies, serve on review teams, and advise on parole-related issues when programs or policies affected people under supervision.

When the Less Is More bill, which allows people doing well on parole to be rewarded with time off their parole terms, incentivizing rules compliance was being developed, I was asked to provide input on implementation.

Unfortunately, DOCCS didn't send parole staff with lived experience, or anyone from their legal department to assist in drafting the law language—only Public Employee Federation (PEF) union representatives attended the many meetings, who viewed the bill as a threat to jobs, which was not accurate. NYSDOCCS added nothing to the language in the finalization of the bill, which became law in September 2021. The negligent actions of NYSDOCCS executives and PEF union officials left parole staff at all levels in the dark for six months after the law went into effect, March 1, 2022.

At the final hour, by which NYSDOCCS was required to be in full implementation by July 2022, development of new job titles, job duties, and other adjustments to supervision practices were still not adequately in place, nor were parole staff fully briefed on the law. During this period, I was called both officially and behind the scenes to provide clarity. My role has often been to bring clarity to debates clouded by fear or misinformation.

I've also been consulted on the HALT Solitary Confinement bill and other reforms because of my deep knowledge of NYSDOCCS and how policies affect people in custody and under supervision. Beyond legislation, I've advised justice organizations on strategy, helping them navigate crises. After the tragic death of Robert Brooks in November 2024, I received calls from both law enforcement organizations and community-based groups seeking guidance on how they should respond. My ability to work across agencies—and the trust I've earned in both spaces—speaks volumes.

I've always chosen to be a problem solver, not just a critic. That's why I'm trusted not only by community groups but also by persons in the city and state government. I take pride in being one of the few people who were tied to a law enforcement agency who is also welcomed and trusted in advocacy spaces. While I don't agree with everything DOCCS does, I know real change requires someone willing to sit at the table and push for solutions.

My advocacy has taken me everywhere—from government offices to candlelight vigils outside the governor's mansion. I'll never forget one frigid December evening in 2018 or 2019, when David and I drove upstate for a clemency vigil. The cold pierced through my boots, and each word we spoke drifted like smoke into the night air. Yet standing with families and advocates, holding candles for women seeking clemency, remains one of the most profound experiences of my life. People were surprised to see me there, but to me, advocacy means showing up, shoulder to shoulder—wherever the fight is.

Every year, advocates local and across the country gather at national events to share, reflect, and recharge. Beyond the Bars and Citizens Against Recidivism are two spaces I regularly support. These aren't just conferences— they're gatherings of people doing the work, reporting back from the front lines, and fueling each other with intelligence, resilience, and heart.

Since its inception in 2011, I've attended the Center for Justice at Columbia University's Beyond the Bars conference. What began as a one-day event organized by a student whose father was incarcerated has grown into a nationally recognized movement. Kathy B. and Missy helped shape it into a space where legal system reform work isn't only discussed but deeply felt. Every spring, it brings together students, faculty, activists, practitioners, and directly impacted people to connect, galvanize, and build toward justice and equity. It's more than a conference—it's a community. Through panels, workshops, performances, and healing spaces, it centers justice on prevention, healing, and transformation.

One unforgettable moment was the 10th Anniversary Memorial Celebration of Eddie Ellis, held in July 2024 at the Schomburg Center and led by his daughter, Greer. Eddie, a pioneer of prison abolition and justice reform, left a legacy that filled the room with purpose. That day felt like a spiritual call to action for criminal justice reformers. Everyone you could imagine—frontliners, backliners, and those in between—was present. The energy was electric, as if the ancestors themselves had summoned us to receive our next instructions.

Through video clips and shared memories, we witnessed Eddie's voice, vision, and unwavering commitment. The room overflowed with Black and Brown folks, young and old, seasoned advocates, and new leaders. We stood together, shoulder to shoulder, reminded of why we do this work. It was an affirmation: progress has been made, but the journey is far from over.

When I enter advocacy spaces and see my comrades—some bruised, some aging, some weary—I'm reminded of our resilience. Despite discomfort, despite the years, we continue to show up. We pour into each other, knowing the fight is far from done. We stand on the principles of leaders gone too soon—Eddie Ellis, Kathy Boudin, Mujahid Farid, Larry White, and so many others who paved the way.

Carceral punishment remains a driving force in U.S. society, with devastating consequences for families and communities—especially Black, Brown, Indigenous, queer, trans, and poor people. While justice movements have made strides, the work is unfinished, and the struggle to confront violence inside prisons and in our communities continues to demand our collective courage.

I don't need to be front and center at every rally or event. What matters is that my support makes a difference. Over the years, countless organizations have asked me to lend my voice—whether co-signing an op-ed, drafting one myself, or strategizing behind the scenes. Even before journalism school, I co-authored pieces with justice leaders to amplify reform. Each request affirms that my words, my work, and my reputation for truth and consistency have carried weight across decades.

Today, I see a new generation of advocates rising. Many of us who've been in this fight for years are getting older, and there's urgency in mentoring younger comrades. The struggle for justice and reform must go on. And as long as I have a voice, I will use it—not for recognition, but to push for real change.

Chapter 13
Loving Through the End

Nothing was the Same

"Saying goodbye didn't happen all at once. It came in moments—small and shattering. Because once he was gone, everything was different. Everything."

That quote captures exactly what I felt when I lost my husband. The goodbye stretched across days, and when it was over, nothing was the same.

Wednesday, April 8, 2020. Everything changed.

A week prior, David said he wasn't feeling well. He couldn't keep anything down and thought it was a stomach virus, so he stayed home from work. For anyone who knew him, this was unusual. He never got sick. And even if he did, he was the type to push through and still show up to work. But that day, he stayed home. I didn't think much of it at the time. The weather was still cool—not quite spring—so maybe he had caught some kind of bug. David worked in a health center with patients; anything was possible.

The symptoms lingered all week. By midweek, I stopped by the Mount Vernon Neighborhood Health Center in Westchester and mentioned his symptoms to one of the doctors. He said it sounded like a stomach virus and recommended fluids and rest. Nothing alarming.

On Saturday, April 4, we drove to BJ's in Monroe, NY. David had been inside the house all week, and I thought fresh air might help. When we arrived, I got out of the car expecting him to follow, but he said he'd stay in the car. That's when I knew something was really wrong—David always liked going into stores. This wasn't just a stomach bug. A full week had passed, and he still felt awful.

I went inside, picked up a few things, and came back out. Then I said, "Let's go to the Bear Mountain COVID testing site." I knew appointments were required, but I decided to try anyway. I told them we had one, and luckily, their computer system was down. They let us drive up the hill, where testing was being done in the Bear Mountain State Park parking lot, while in our car.

This was the height of the COVID-19 pandemic. People were terrified, streets were empty, and every store—except for food and pharmacies—was closed. Neighbors peeked through blinds, afraid to step outside. The world felt like it was holding its breath.

David was tested, and we went back home. He rested through the weekend, still not feeling better.

By Tuesday, April 7, around 11:30 a.m., he was getting dressed so we could go out. He went to the car to grab something and suddenly felt lightheaded. He sat down on the hallway floor. I wasn't home—I was on my way back. Someone from our building called to tell me he was sitting in the hall, not feeling well.

I was just about to get off Exit 14A (Airmont) on the New York State Thruway. We lived only two minutes away. When I got home, he was still sitting on the floor. The ambulance had already been called. Shortly after I arrived, EMTs came, checked his vitals, and placed him in the ambulance.

They told me to call Good Samaritan Hospital in Suffern, NY, in two to three hours for an update. I agreed. As they closed the ambulance doors, David and I exchanged our last words: "I love you." It was around 1 p.m.

I called the hospital at 4 p.m., as instructed. The ER doctor said David had labored breathing. They asked if he wanted to go on a ventilator, and he said yes. That's when the gravity of the situation hit me. The test results from Saturday still hadn't come back, but whatever he had was moving fast.

The doctor said they were running more tests and told me to call back later for an update.

Around 8 p.m., another doctor called—a woman this time. She said David's organs were shutting down and that if I wanted to see him, I needed to come immediately.

Thank God we lived in Rockland County. Good Samaritan Hospital wasn't following the same strict visitation restrictions as hospitals in New York City. I was allowed to go.

About 15 minutes after the hospital called, the testing site finally confirmed: David was positive for COVID-19. After the call, the room went dark. My mind went blank. I was still in shock.

Even though I had feared this possibility, nothing prepared me for the reality. At the height of COVID-19, no one really knew what was going on. Symptoms varied. Treatments were experimental. Everything was uncertain. If David survived, it would be nothing short of a miracle.

I called my daughter to tell her I was on my way to the hospital. I wasn't sure if they would let her in, but I said she could try if she wanted. By the time she arrived from New Jersey, it was around 9:30 p.m.

At the hospital, I began calling family members, though I can't recall exactly who I reached. I got Tyra, his daughter, who lives in Connecticut. I tried calling his son but couldn't get through. I believe I also reached his nephew, Talent. I explained what was happening, and they were able to say a prayer and speak to David, even though he was already on the ventilator and couldn't respond.

The hospital allowed my daughter in for a brief time. I've always believed that very sick people sometimes hold on, not for themselves, but for the ones they love—the ones they fear will fall apart without them. When I saw David, I was shaken by the ventilator mask taped to his face. I knew how much he hated hospitals, hated being sick, hated taking medicine.

I leaned in and said, "I know you don't want to be here. I know you're very sick. And as much as I want you to hold on and let God do what only God can do, I also understand if you need to surrender. If you're tired, I'll be okay. It'll be hard, but I'll be okay." As much as I am a planner and always stay prepared, there was no preparation for this type of conversation I needed to have with the love of my life, my everything.

When my daughter came in, I shared my belief that sometimes people need permission to let go. I told her she might need to give her Papa permission if he needed it. Her response broke my heart: "I'm not lying to Papa. I'm not going to be all right." And I respected that.

A few moments later, she went to the bathroom. When she came back, her eyes were red from crying. She stood beside him and said, "Papa, I'm not going to be all right. But I don't want to see you like this either."

The room fell silent.

Then the nurses came in and told us he was being moved to the ICU. Only one person could go. My daughter went home, and I went upstairs with him. Initially, the nurse supervisor said I could only stay 15 minutes. But the attending nurse allowed 45 minutes because the supervisor went on a lunch break. I left around 1 a.m., consumed with thoughts of David—how much he hated being in that condition—and wondering what he and God had decided.

Around 1 p.m. the next day, the hospital called. David had passed.

As soon as I got off the call, I began reaching out to the kids—his son David, his daughters Tyra and Tanika —and other family members to share the news. That afternoon, I organized a Zoom meeting with relatives who were near and far, California, Virginia, Georgia, South Carolina, Mount Vernon, New York. We did what Sewards do: we came together.

We prayed. We laughed. We planned. Love and support flowed freely. We leaned on one another the way we always had.

But what weighed heavily on me was the grief I felt from Tyra and little David. They had just lost their mother, and now they were grieving their father. I tried to imagine losing both parents in such a short time. Grief doesn't care how old you are. Everyone carries it differently. I learned that firsthand through my own journey when my grandmother and best friend passed.

Once we caught our breath, the next question was: would I be able to give David a proper homegoing service? Or would the last image of him—hooked up to machines in the ICU—be the one that stayed with me forever?

My mind went into overdrive. I started calling funeral homes in Mount Vernon. David was born and raised there, and most of his family and friends still lived in the area. I finally reached Leewood Funeral Home and made an appointment. Tyra met me there, and together we made the arrangements.

Having just gone through this with her mother, Tyra was a tremendous help. She offered practical advice—like ordering extra death certificates through the funeral home, which saved time and money. Her wisdom and strength meant so much to me. We leaned on each other during that painful time.

Soon after, I held another family Zoom. Since David passed in April, we decided his homegoing service would be on his birthday—April 22, 2020. We brought everyone together again to plan the service. With COVID-19 still raging, travel was limited, so we knew the homegoing had to be accessible virtually.

My cousin Sheila and her daughter Chanel created the program. Everyone sent photos and memories. My brother's first wife, Cheryl, authored a beautiful poem we included. The love and contributions poured in from everywhere.

Because of the funeral home's restrictions, only five people were allowed in the viewing room at a time. I reached out to people close to me who knew David—some I'd met during their incarceration, others after—and asked for help. They showed up. Simmons recruited two others to manage the flow of people—five entering one door, five exiting another.

Missy, my dear friend, came to videotape the service. My granddaughter, Chey, and Tyra created a tribute video with old-school music and oversaw the virtual production. David loved old-school—the Stylistics, the Whispers, the Temptations, and so many others.

David could sing his heart out. On trips down south, he sang all the way down I-95. When I walked the compound at Orleans Correctional Facility, David and others would stop me on the grounds—or come to my office in the gym building—and sing a piece of an old-school song. "I Wanna Know Your Name" by the Intruders was my favorite.

We also wanted everyone to have a mask. Maritza, my other daughter, who is my daughter's best friend, had a friend who made personalized ones. I ordered enough for all who attended and those who couldn't. They said "Goose" and "Stay Six Feet." We placed them in Ziploc bags with gloves and a prayer card—a safety measure and a keepsake.

David was known for his style. At 6'6", he walked with pride and commanded attention. He was a sharp dresser—always clean, coordinated, and wearing cologne that often made men and women stop to ask its name. My husband was an OG, a true original gangster who had transformed his life completely.

In his casket, he wore a blue suit, his favorite Kangol hat, and Gucci shades. He had a toothpick in his mouth—just like always. A deck of cards in his hand. Dice on the ledge. And in the corner, a pint of corn liquor—because half of Mount Vernon knew that was his drink of choice.

He looked as though he were only sleeping. Fine and dapper as always.

That peaceful image helped. He hadn't suffered long, sparing us the trauma of a slow decline. But then something happened that none of us expected—his right eye began to tear. It was as if he were crying. Everyone felt it. It moved us all.

Despite the circumstances, the viewing went smoothly. The funeral home never had to intervene. Everything was orderly, respectful, and full of love.

On the day of the funeral, the weather was beautiful. The sun was shining brightly, the sky was clear, and though a little windy, it was warm enough to hold the service outside on the steps of the funeral home. Family, friends, and people passing by stood in the street, spaced out, listening.

My nephew Derrick led the service. Other family members participated in various parts. And I wrote and read David's obituary.

Although many people could have told the story of Goose—his nickname—I was the only one who could truly tell the story of David. I made sure to include everything. He sold clothes, cologne, and other things. He knew the hustle. People borrowed money from him, and yes, he charged interest. I reminded everyone that day—just in case they were wondering—that their debts were cleared. That brought a laugh.

What was most remarkable that day was the tribute from David's son's coworkers. He worked for the City of Mount Vernon, a parade of city trucks from the sanitation and water department, honking as they drove past the funeral home. People on the street stopped and stared, wondering who could be so important that a sea of city trucks would roll through Mount Vernon in salute. That person was my husband, David.

As I said previously, he was like the mayor of Mount Vernon. He knew everyone, and everyone knew him. The Seward name was well-known, and that day, the outpouring of love touched me deeply.

Because of COVID-19, we knew many people who lived locally would not be able to attend. We also mapped out a funeral procession route and shared it with friends and family. We asked people to come outside along the route and wear burgundy and gold—David's school colors—as a sign of respect. About 25 cars and motorcycles joined the procession.

We left Leewood Funeral Home and passed by his workplace at the Mount Vernon Neighborhood Health Center. As we turned onto 4th Street, the entire staff—doctors, nurses, clerical workers, even the CEO—stood outside holding balloons and signs, sending their love and prayers.

We stopped, and I was able to hug them and hand out one of the large photo posters we had displayed at the funeral home. It was something you could hardly imagine. It was beautiful.

After the procession, some people went home, but a few of us went to City Island, one of David's favorite places. Johnny's Reef was open, and since we could not have a traditional repast, I treated those who joined us to lunch. It was simple, but it meant something.

Despite all the obstacles COVID-19 presented, I truly believe we gave David one of the best homegoing services possible. Family from across the country—from Mount Vernon to California—were virtually able to attend. Everyone said it was beautiful. And I agree. It was.

We made it happen in a time when the world was standing still. David was laid to rest with dignity and pride. He came full circle—from being seen as a menace in the Mount Vernon neighborhood to becoming a champion of the community. The love and support from family and friends were priceless.

I thank God every day—for allowing me to see my husband in the hospital, to plan his funeral, to give him a proper farewell. I will never forget the last words we said to each other: "I love you."

There was a period when I became afraid. Older people would say, "Once everything settles down, once the business is handled, it'll hit you." I did not understand what they meant. What exactly was going to hit me?

So, I decided to prepare myself. I do not do well with surprises. I reached out to a pastor friend of mine, Reverend Shannon from Brooklyn. I had heard he did grief counseling. At first, he was hesitant—because we had been friends for a long time, and he wanted to be sure he could serve me well. Eventually, he agreed, and I am so grateful that he did. I do not think I could have done it with anyone else.

We met virtually for eight weeks. COVID-19 was still raging. The death toll was on the news every day. Funeral homes and hospitals were renting refrigerated trucks because they could not manage the number of deceased people. It was a time none of us will ever forget.

You couldn't tell David and me that the song "Stars" by Kindred the Family Soul wasn't written for us. Even now, it finds me in the moments when I'm thinking of my husband. Most recently, while in Puerto Rico on my way to the fort Castillo de San Cristobal in Old San Juan, where his ashes rest, the song came up on my playlist. I just smiled and whispered, "David, I'm on my way."

Lyrics:

"So many times you could have walked away, but I never had to beg you to stay. You knew it, and I knew it— what we had was real. We kept learning, kept growing, and our love deepened with each passing day. I watched you get better at this—at us—and each moment only convinced me more. We trusted love, took the risk, ran at our own pace, and won our own race. I could never have turned away. We

have come so far. The stars look down at you, and my heart belongs right here, always next to you…"

I did grief counseling once a week. It was informative, and I learned a lot. Reverend Shannon, I think, learned a few things too. One session focused on something called the academy performance—the idea that when people ask how you are doing, you should answer with how you are actually feeling. I struggled with that concept. I did not feel obligated to tell people, especially those I did not know well or who could not truly support me, how I was really feeling. If someone could not pour into me what I needed in that moment, why should I open up? Especially about something as sacred as the loss of my husband.

When I shared that perspective with Reverend Shannon, he admitted he had never heard it framed that way. But he understood. While I appreciated his validation, I did not need it. I knew I had a point. Not everyone is equipped to hold space for your grief. And I was not going to be someone's emotional guinea pig—letting them believe they were helping when, in truth, their words felt hollow.

The sessions were powerful. They made me realize how many people approach grief from a cookie-cutter perspective—because that is what they were taught. It is a learned behavior. I have seen people lower their voices, slow their speech, and adopt a somber tone when talking about someone's death—even if they barely knew the person. I would ask, "Did you know them?" and they would reply, "Oh no, that was my cousin's sister's friend." And I would think, Why are you acting like you lost your first cousin?

People would say, "I wanted to call, but I didn't know what to say." In my mind, all they needed to say was, "Hello. How are you?" That was it. Nothing more. Just show up. Just be present.

I also learned it was okay to stop answering the phone. Some called with good intentions but did not realize they were imposing, asking me to rehash the details of David's passing when I was not ready. I learned to protect my peace.

My mom, my daughter, and I cleaned out the Rockland, New York apartment. David, as everyone knew, was a dresser. He had furs, suits, and a serious cologne and watch collection. I made sure his son, nephews, and other family members received his clothes. His colognes were shared, too.

A few months before he passed, David had said to me, "If anything happens to me, make sure you check my pockets before you give any of my stuff away." I brushed it off at the time, but I remembered. That is why I only had a handful of people helping me go through his things—we had to check every pocket.

And sure enough, in the pocket of a jacket he had not worn in who knows how long, I found $5,000 in cash. I laughed. That was David. He did not trust banks. He did things his way. Thank God there was no fire—he would have fainted knowing his money burned up. But I was grateful.

At the time, I was scheduled to renew my car lease. When I arrived at the dealership, the deposit they requested was $5,000. I handed it over and said, "He's still looking out for his Boo." That was David. Always prepared. Always providing.

He was never truly broke. When he said he was broke, he meant he did not want to spend what he had. He was money-conscious, a saver, a hustler. He could sell anything. He took his "unlicensed pharmaceutical behavior" and turned it into something more legal and marketable— clothes, accessories, whatever people needed. He had charm, customer service skills, and a way of engaging people that was uniquely his.

Meanwhile, I gave up my Rockland County residence and became a full-time resident of Queens.

For the first three years after David's passing, I honored his birthday with family gatherings. The first year, we did a butterfly release. Butterflies were sent to our families in Delaware, Virginia, North Carolina, South Carolina, and New York. Everyone released them in their memory and shared videos.

The second year, we did a dove and balloon release, followed by dinner at a local restaurant in Mount Vernon. The third year, we gathered at a wine bar for another balloon release and shared a bit to eat.

Each of those three years, I also hosted a continental breakfast at his job for the staff in his memory. But by the fourth year, I stopped. At some point, I had to lay him to rest—not just physically, but emotionally. It became overwhelming, trying to make it right and ensure everyone felt included. It was a lot.

I realized that memorializing him for those three years was more than most people do. And now, on his birthday, I try to relax. I will do something for myself. Something that lets him know he is missed, but never a burden. Because David would never want to be a burden.

When I want to hear his voice, I replay The Skin Deep video on YouTube (3.6K likes): "Formerly Incarcerated

Husband Admits Biggest Regret | {THE AND} Vanda & David."

Transcript (excerpt):

Q: What are your three favorite memories you share?

My Response: When we first got married in Mount McGregor Correctional Facility, we were in the chapel. When you started singing, all of the guys there… Well, let me back up. When they realized they were about to witness a wedding, even though they were all wearing green, they tucked in their shirts and buttoned their collars. Then, when you began to sing, they all joined in. That was one of my favorite memories.

The second was when we flew to Hawaii. It was your first time flying, and every five minutes you asked, "What's that?" They gave you those little wings they usually give to kids. Later, when we went to eat in the crater of an active volcano for lunch, we could see the sulfur rising through the windows. You had no idea I was taking you to an active volcano. I think that was when you realized your wife is a little crazy.

Q: How do you describe me to others?

David's Response: That's easy. I am your biggest fan, and it is easy for me to tell people about all you have accomplished and how much you have succeeded in life. You inspire others. Everyone who knows you can see how you empower those around you, and I think that is one of your best qualities. I love you deeply for that.

Q: When are you proudest of me?

My Response: I am proudest of you when you take time to truly engage with your kids. There are so many things that make me proud. You have been home for 26 years, at the same job, proving yourself to be an asset, never once thinking about going back to jail or any kind of institution. That makes me proud because I know the reality of recidivism, and here you are—a man who did more than one bid—coming home and knowing change was the only way forward.

I am proud that you said you were not going back and were determined, by hook or by crook, to stay free. That is something you should be proud of, too, especially knowing how stacked the cards are.

David's Response: You have also taught me a lot. You gave me a different mindset. And when it comes to the kids, you always said we had to build our own relationships with them. From day one, I loved Tyra. I nicknamed our baby girl and had already accepted her as part of me. All I wanted was to build with her—to be the best I could be for her, to be there when she needed me.

When I went away, my kids were kids. When I came home, they were adults. That is what I miss the most—not being there for them at all. But I still have time.

Q: Why do you love me?

David's Response: Let me count the ways. I love you for you. I have always loved you for you. You would think after 28 years we would have cried all the tears we could, but no—our love just runs deep.

Chapter 14
After the Storm

Take a Deep Breath

"Widowhood wasn't a title I asked for. But it followed me everywhere—even into spaces I never thought I'd enter. And when I found myself in rooms where change was happening, I realized—I wasn't just surviving grief. I was carrying his legacy, too."

These words capture exactly how I felt as I began navigating life without David. There is nothing more priceless than knowing that the last time you saw someone alive, you told them you loved them, and they heard you, and understood you. That moment is etched in my heart. Always and forever, I will love David.

David and I loved Puerto Rico. It was our sanctuary—serene, peaceful, grounding. We walked its streets, browsed the shops, blended in with tourists without really being tourists. We moved through those spaces as if we belonged.

During the COVID-19 pandemic, I took one of his urns and flew there with my daughter and her girlfriend, Maritza. We brought his ashes to the waters below Castillo de San Cristobal, a historic fortress in Old San Juan. Later, on a private sunset cruise, we stopped at the perfect spot, said a prayer, and released the urn into the sea.

His ashes rest in many places, but in my heart, his spirit lives in Puerto Rico—a place we both loved deeply.

Not long after, I acquired a second home there: a three-bedroom penthouse right on the beach. I returned every month—sometimes alone, sometimes with my daughter. It became a place of peace, healing, and remembrance.

One year, I celebrated my birthday in Puerto Rico with three of my girlfriends, my daughter, and my other daughter, Martiza. It became my refuge to relax, regroup, and release. My daughter and I moved about as if we had been born and raised there, just as David and I once had. At night, my daughter and Maritza would often get shooed from the main floor by me because they liked to make noise after 10 p.m. They'd head up to the penthouse level with their rosé and music. During COVID, a DJ hosted virtual parties, and they'd dance, record videos, and get shout-outs from him. That was their nightly ritual.

We visited often, even during the height of the pandemic. I remember arriving at hotels where staff sprayed bags with alcohol. At Walmart and Home Depot, employees stood at entrances, sanitizing carts and hands. Precautions were strict—stricter than many places in the States. By 8 p.m., everything closed—restaurants, bars, even Walmart. You just had enough time to get what you needed and get home.

But the pandemic didn't stop us. You might think that after such a traumatic loss, we would have shut ourselves in, locked the doors, and stayed still. But we didn't. We kept moving. We kept living.

Back home, my daughter and I created our own rituals. We treated Target like an outing—browsing the aisles, trying things on, making it an adventure. Sometimes she'd drive to a Target in New Jersey just to walk around. I'd do the same in Long Island, wandering the aisles to stay out of the house. It was our way of not letting grief swallow us whole.

During that time, I also asked myself what else I wanted to do, how I wanted to live. I was still Director of the Criminal Justice Program at Kingsborough Community College, still putting myself in spaces where I could grow in my craft. I stayed busy. I kept learning.

I was adjusting to a new normal—life without my husband of 28 years. My travel buddy. Let's go check this out, partner. My biggest cheerleader. My everything.

He had been my daughter's papa, his kids' dad, an uncle, a cousin, a brother-in-law. Now, navigating those relationships without him felt different, even strange. But I felt him everywhere I went.

I feel him still, moving around me as I put my life back in order. Many people don't know this, but I go to a card reader. Before she even knew David had passed, she said, "There's a tall, dark-skinned man around you. He's here now." She described David exactly.

I feel him especially on the days I don't want to do anything, when I just want to lie in bed and watch TV, without moving or thinking. I hear his voice in my head saying, "Girl, if you don't get your ass up and handle your business."

And that voice keeps me going. It pushes me forward.

Even though it's been over five years now, nothing has "hit me" the way people warned it would. Maybe it's still lurking, waiting. I don't know. But I believe the reason it hasn't crushed me is that I had a good marriage. We left each other in a good space. I have no woulda, coulda, shoulda. No regrets. And I'm proud of that.

The storm of losing David was devastating, but what came after wasn't just survival; it was learning to carry his love with me in a new way. In Puerto Rico's sunsets, in my daughter's laughter, in the voice that still tells me to get up and handle my business. The storm passed, but the love remained—transformed into something that could travel with me wherever I chose to go.

Chapter 15
The Work and Love Continues to Call Me

Living My Purpose, Embracing Renewal

"The work never really stopped—it just shifted. From prisons to classrooms to New York State Capitol halls and boardrooms, I carried everything I had lived into every space I entered."

God continues to bless me as I walk this path—educating, supporting, and raising my voice for those who are unheard or misunderstood. I am giving my all and living my truth, fully.

Now that I have laid David to rest and managed every detail, the idea of returning to "normal" feels anything but normal. From here forward, my journey is rooted in ideas, observations, and the purpose that has always guided me: ensuring justice-impacted people are not forgotten, that they are heard, and that I keep pushing the reform agenda forward. Though I retired as a criminal justice professional, I am still living my purpose.

In January 2020, I set out to learn more about juveniles in the justice system. I began supporting a Brooklyn organization that supports young people on probation.

Through this work, I met an extraordinary team of mentors and artists. These mentors, with lived experience, reminded me of my old forensic team from FEGS. Like them, they did fearless mentoring directly on the streets—in East New York, Brownsville, and Bed-Stuy. They were relentless, present, and committed. Their pasts didn't hinder them; instead, their experiences equipped them to walk alongside youth bound by the street code.

Many of these young people came from homes touched by incarceration, substance abuse, or trauma. Yet their parents still loved them, even while facing their own unhealed pain. That is why mentors mattered so deeply. During COVID-19, when schools, services, and public spaces were closed, mentors still showed up—with masks, gloves, and open hearts.

Probation staff in Brooklyn at that time were equally committed, always willing to pilot programs and embrace new ideas for youth. Together, mentors and staff created life-affirming experiences: paintball trips, bowling, Great Adventure, Fright Night, and even dinners at Brooklyn Chop House. Dedicated staff: Freddie, Kenya, Lyndell, Desire, Chicken Wing, Gus, Damon, Shamel. Dr. Patterson, Merky, and Monique are a stellar team armed with grit, heart, and hustle.

When New York City Probation launched a video contest on social distancing during the height of COVID, the Brooklyn Arches group—alongside videographer Sampson S. and me created an opportunity for young people to write a script about social distancing. The young people also filmed and starred in the video. Their video won the contest, and it was broadcast citywide on LINKNYC kiosks located near subway stations and street corner information kiosks. Producing that video gave them purpose in a dark time.

Later, we created "What Young People Want from Adults." Young people from the Brooklyn Arches program interviewed strangers in Union Square Park and asked the adults what they think young people expect from adults. After the taping, a video was produced, and the message was clear: young people want adults to act like adults, not imitate them by dressing and talking like a young person. That project sparked powerful reflections and ended with a public screening. These moments gave them voice, pride, and visibility.

But working with youth also revealed harsh realities. I once overheard a mother say she should have swallowed her daughter because she couldn't get her daughter's girlfriend food stamps. I was stunned. Another time, a mother threatened to call the police on her son—just a day before his probation ended—because he refused to give her his child's Social Security number to use on her tax filing so she could get a larger tax refund check. Thankfully, he had the presence of mind to record the exchange, and I was able to intervene with probation and Bronx Defenders. His charges were dropped.

These experiences reinforced what I already knew: not all troubled youth come from troubled homes, but some do—and sometimes, the harm starts at home. That is why mentors matter.

Although I knew that restorative justice was a powerful model, my in-depth engagement with Dr. Patterson enhanced my knowledge and reinforced that this model should be used not only for young people but also for adults. Yet New York prisons and jails rarely apply it. Incarcerated individuals often want to make amends and apologize for their harm, but the NYS Department of Corrections and Community Supervision directive #4422 is very restrictive. This directive prohibits any communication, even if voluntary and facilitated by a neutral third party. It also blocks victims- and the person who caused harm- from voluntarily engaging in dialogue programs, which are a cornerstone of restorative justice. This is a lost opportunity for healing on both sides.

After years of working with adults, it was refreshing to witness that same passion I have with adults directed toward youth that Dr. Patterson and her team carried with them every day. The team's impact stretched far beyond the block—whether in detention centers or family homes. No matter where the young person was, the support remained steady.

I have also long believed in knowing your professional strengths and limits. Over time, I realized I was not suited to work with domestic violence survivors or young people in deep crisis. It was not from lack of care, but because I lacked the specialized skill set and emotional stamina required. It is important to know when to step back and let others lead.

I left that space with a lasting bond with Dr. Patterson, a woman who has dedicated herself to young people and their families. I respect her deeply—a powerful Black woman who returned to school as an adult, a wife, and a mother, earning her PhD. That kind of determination matters, especially in the criminal justice arena.

Personal Challenges and Changes

COVID-19 also brought personal changes. I realized my mother, who was 90 years young, needed more care, and my oldest grandson, Chris, needed more guidance. He had been living with her, but during the same week I buried David, it became clear I had to step in. I moved Mommy in with me, then later moved her to assisted living in Ardsley, NY. She liked it—it was beautiful—but as her condition worsened and she once wandered off the premises, I then decided to bring her back to the Bronx, where she could receive better services.

In April 2024, she suffered a stroke. It was devastating; she had always been healthy. After nearly 100 days in rehab, I brought her home with 24-hour care. With good aides and my grandson Chris, who lives with me, and assists around the house, we made it work. My mom is now in a wheelchair and has lost use of her right hand, but for over a year, Mommy has been doing well, and she still has a sense of humor. In November, she celebrated her 95th birthday, which she told me she turned 22 years old. She is still sassy and quick with her verbal comeback. As long as she continues with her sass and wit, I know she is doing well.

During this time, I was also asked to consider joining the New York State Parole Board as one of the commissioners. I completed the process for endorsement, though I knew there were hesitations. Some feared I would release everyone—a misconception about my approach to justice. My record speaks otherwise. Others may have feared my independence. I am not beholden to any agency, and that makes me harder to control. That is unsettling to some people.

The DOCCS Commissioner Opportunity

After I became a widow—a word I never used until I updated my bio—someone suggested I include the line: "Widow after 28 years of marriage." I hesitated because I dislike labels; they box you in and dictate expectations. But as I worked to establish my presence in the community, I realized my story, including my loss, was part of who I am.

Not long after, I was approached about considering the role of Commissioner of the New York State Department of Corrections and Community Supervision (DOCCS) after the retirement of Acting Commissioner Anthony Annucci. Advocacy groups rallied behind me, pushing for change and hoping the Senate would not confirm the current commissioner, Daniel Martuscello III. I knew I was qualified, and I was ready to step in.

My first order of business was to make sure the governor and other state legislators were aware that I was interested in the Commissioner position. Many felt that my efforts to inform people of my interest in this position gave the impression that I was running a campaign, but that was never the case. It was about transparency—making sure legislators and the public knew the position was open and that other qualified candidates existed. These roles are rarely publicized, so I took the initiative. I handed out my resume during caucus weekend in Albany to lawmakers and sent out emails of interest as well. My efforts did not go unseen. I received some endorsements, but not enough. A local Albany news reporter told me during a conversation that my name was in the legislative and governors' spaces.

I was warned by my mentors and colleagues that if chosen, I would need strong security that did not include NYSDOCCS officers. Being a Black woman in that role would upset the status quo. I understood the risks, and I was ready. If that was how my story was meant to end, I had made peace with it.

Still, politics prevailed. The Senate confirmed the acting commissioner, Daniel Martuscello III, a man who had been in the department his entire career, who grew up in the system, yet never pushed it forward. Like so many before him, he simply fell in line. Taxpayers and those impacted by the system are left with the same old cycle—same story, different day.

What frustrated me most was the hypocrisy. Legislators who supported me in private turned around and praised him in public. Watching them flip like that was disheartening, but that is politics. And that is why I am not a politician. I tell people the truth. I prepare my teams for change instead of keeping them in the dark. I have always believed people manage change better when you bring them along early. I live by that. And no matter what titles I hold—or do not hold—I will continue to live in truth, push for justice, and center the people too often left unheard.

The Fixer

Safe Space, Strong Shoulders

Over the decades, I have been a safe space for people— my family, and those who became like family. I opened my doors to my cousin Stacey, who was struggling at home and battling addiction, and let her stay with me until she was ready to move on.

I've welcomed relatives from the South who came to New York while facing legal concerns. I've taken in family members and crew members—whether they were headed to rehab or simply trying to navigate the challenges of life on the streets.

Friends and family often came to me for several reasons; they could no longer stay in their own homes. That safe place was usually mine. It's not as though I advertised myself that way, but my nonjudgmental, open, and trustworthy nature made people feel they could turn to me. I was once even called "the fixer" because people—family, friends, in-laws, and others—knew they could call me, and I would help them sort things out. And it wasn't always criminal justice-related.

One of the most memorable times I was called to help was when I was the director at FEGS. A young woman who worked for me, and whom I had taken under my wing, confided in me about her domestic violence situation. She told me she was tired of her mother pressuring her to marry her children's father, even though he was abusive. She hadn't told her mother about the abuse. I advised her that the only way her mother would stop pushing for the marriage was if she told her the truth—outside of heated moments, in a calm setting.

A few weeks later, she followed my advice. She told her mother. Soon after, I attended an after-work all-girls event with my staff and her sisters. One of her sisters pulled me aside and said, "Mama assembled us on Sunday and told us we had to get my sister's man out of the house by this Sunday. And Mama said to let you know."

That Sunday, he was gone—packed up and out, as if the marshal had come. Coming from a small family myself, it amazed me to see how a large family could mobilize so quickly, carrying out their mother's orders with precision. What struck me even more was that her Mother wanted me to know and trusted me to help keep things steady. That moment has always stayed with me.

I often ask myself: What am I doing—or not doing—that makes people feel I'm the one they can turn to? I know I possess knowledge and instincts from different corners of life, but much of what I do feels instinctive. I don't always know why—I just act.

I recall my time as executive director of ComAlert at the Brooklyn DA's Office. One of the representatives from the Doe Fund came into my office years later, saw my degrees on the wall, and said, "I knew you were smart. You've got the edge of the street, but there was something about you that told me you weren't all street." We both laughed. Comments like that have followed me for years.

I don't usually discuss my personal life or academic accomplishments. I don't give out names; I'll say, "my daughter," "my husband," or "my grandchild." I remember at my retirement party when my secretary smiled after I told her David would take her to the Amtrak train. She said, "Can I ask you a question? Whose David?" She had only ever heard me call him "husband." Protecting my family has always been important. Safeguarding them became second nature — because no matter how much people like me or value my work, I don't take chances. When it comes to my family, no one is exempt. That instinct comes from both my time in the streets and the professional roles I've held.

I've always sought to learn from spaces where justice-impacted people gather. I remember going with my girlfriend Pat to a writer's event upstate, near Connecticut. We didn't know it was on a farm. It was summer, and we arrived in maxi dresses and flip-flops—definitely not "farm cute." The event was held in a barn with bales of hay for seating, which poked through our dresses. It was funny, but unforgettable.

Later, I had the opportunity to attend a summer retreat at the same farm—a few days of writing, reflection, and nature. It was peaceful: birds chirping, bonfires at night, family-style meals. The only thing I didn't love was the kale. It was kale season, and every meal included something with kale. To this day, I don't eat kale because it reminds me of that farm!

Beyond those experiences, I've filled my life with criminal justice events, both personal and professional. In order to educate the next generation of criminal justice professionals, every year at the end of the Spring semester, I accompany my students to the Eastern State Penitentiary Museum in Philadelphia. The students learned so much and have had the opportunity to network with other Kingsborough students and faculty.

I love visiting and learning about different prisons. What the students did not know was that I could spend all day there. Most recently, a few hand-picked criminal justice students, Professor Brown, and I participated in "The Drive." All persons who participate in the Drive visit a person who has spent decades in prison. Many who receive limited to no visits or have minimal communication with friends and family. The students and I visited for about 2 hours, speaking with someone incarcerated.

The conversations included asking about their carceral experiences and discussing the students' career goals with hopes of getting some insight into what makes a good criminal justice professional. This was an experience that they will never forget.

After the visiting experience, they were enlightened and were amazed that the person they were sitting across from was nothing like the textbook or movies describe. Our visit also had an impact on the people we visited. The wife of the gentleman I visited knew the organizer of "The Drive" and wanted to know who I was. So, I emailed her.

Her response covered a lot, but the two memorable statements that stood out were "I cannot express how meaningful it was to read your reflections on your visit with my husband. Knowing that you took time out of your day—especially in such extreme cold—to show up with empathy, care, and openness means more to our family than words can adequately convey," and "I am especially grateful that you brought your students to the prison. Creating opportunities for future criminal justice professionals to step inside a prison, engage in real conversations, and truly humanize incarcerated people is so powerful. Experiences like that can shift perspectives in lasting ways, and I deeply respect your commitment to educating students through compassion, lived experience, and truth."

If all goes well, it is my plan to incorporate this prison educational outing twice a year. As it has been said, I eat, sleep, and breathe criminal justice. Which is true, I am passionate about all aspects of the criminal justice system and legal system reforms. There is never a time when I say I know it all because I do not. I am always trying to enhance my knowledge.

You would think that after decades of being directly involved with the prison system, spending time in a visiting room would not be anything major. That is so far from the truth. Not only was it emotional watching the families embrace their loved ones when they entered the visiting room, but one of the guys my student was visiting recognized my name and said he was just listening to something where I was the speaker. As I left the visiting area, the snacks we had not eaten, I gave them to other visitors on the way out. Then, a family that saw me giving away snacks handed me a KitKat and said, 'Thank you.' As strange as it may seem, that was the best Saturday I have had in a while, despite leaving home at 5:00 in the morning to standing outside on a line with others in the frigid cold of 19 degrees. The passion I've acquired about the justice system, and being a criminal justice professor, allows me to share with a new generation of criminal justice professionals' experiences that go beyond the text and class lecture.

I've dedicated my entire adult life to the carceral system and to people impacted by it. And while I don't always know why people see me as a safe space, I know I've carried that role proudly, consistently, and with love.

Voices from My Journey

Throughout the writing of this memoir, I often reached out to people who had been part of my life during moments that felt blurred or incomplete in my memory. I hoped their recollections might fill the gaps—or awaken memories I had buried or forgotten. I contacted family, friends, and even unexpected voices from my past, asking them to share what they remembered.

The responses were overwhelming—raw, heartfelt, detailed, and sometimes surprising. Their words didn't just revive the past; they grounded me, reminding me of who I was, who I've become, and the many lives intertwined with mine. It became clear these voices belonged here. Rather than leave them tucked away in my private notes, I've chosen to include key excerpts because they add depth, truth, and perspective that only those who lived alongside me can provide.

Lila G. (Colleague)

One day, I was at the copy machine making copies of a monthly newsletter listing job openings. I was minding my business when Vanda walked by. She asked, "What are you doing?" I said, "I'm making copies of this newsletter." She replied, "Oh, OK. Make me a copy." I noticed a job that seemed perfect for her and pointed it out. About a week later, I asked if she had applied. She said, "Not yet." Later, she told me she applied—and that moment began her transition from the FEGS NYC Link program to becoming the Executive Director of the ComALERT program.

After that, when people learned I was the one who gave her the newsletter, they said, "You're the reason Vanda is leaving!" I had to bite the bullet and reply, "Maybe it was time for her to move on," even though none of us wanted her to go. But I believe that was the Lord's plan—and it blessed her to move on to even greater things than ComALERT.

Bruce (Nephew)

I remember when you came to Mid-Orange Correctional Facility in 2008. It was my day off, and I was outside in the yard working out when I heard my name called over the P.A. system: "Alfonzo Seward 96A 6126, report to the gymnasium." I thought it was to pick up the newspaper from my boss, who ran the gym. Instead, he told me my aunt was there leading a workshop for the guys incarcerated. At that time, I had already been in prison for 13 years on a 12½ to 25-year sentence for several armed robbery offenses.

When I saw you, and we began to talk—as if I was just seeking help finding a job after release—I was like a happy camper. Seeing a family member in prison is powerful; it helps you stay focused on doing right and preparing for freedom. It was a defining period for me because I was already walking a different path—deep into God and the church, working toward my freedom. Talking with you about family and life prepared me for what was expected outside.

You were, are, and always will be a blessing to my growth. Not only are you educated in so many areas, but I have always seen you as deeply caring. Whatever you touch, you work hard at and succeed. I love how you push people forward if they're willing to learn and do the work. I'm proud to be your nephew, Auntie. I'll never forget the tools, wisdom, and encouraging words you gave me. You were always about your A game, and I love that about you. The world needs more people like you. Hopefully, this sheds a little light on who you are and what you mean to people. Love you, Auntie.

Van C. (Brother of Boobie)

To my dear sister Vanda, although we didn't spend much time together, the quality of it meant everything. From the honest love and compassion you showed my brother to the bond you built with my mother and family, I often thought of you as my older sister—though ironically, I later learned you're younger than me.

Your maturity, compassion, kindness, and willingness to give your heart to friends, loved ones, and the community are something I'll never forget. You are one beautiful Soul Sista. Oh, and did I mention fine and sexy too? All the best, and God bless!

Joe W. (1st Black Superintendent in NYS Department of Correctional Services)

Vanda, over the past thirty years, I've known you ever since the early days of the New York State Minorities in Corrections (NYSMIC), now New York State Minorities in Criminal Justice (NYSMICJ)—you have exemplified true leadership and determination to change the New York State Criminal Justice System from its history as an institution of injustice.

When you entered the Department of Correctional Services in the late 1980s, you stepped into a system still wrestling with the legacy of Attica. I was already part of what I call the first generation of program staff and advocates, determined to provide meaningful rehabilitation services to people who had been profoundly neglected. You, Vanda, became part of the second generation, carrying that mission forward with passion and skill.

As the first Black superintendent in New York State, I had the privilege of leading Fulton and Lincoln Correctional Facilities from 1980 to 2011. Yet some of my greatest pride comes from watching your journey unfold—not only during your years inside correctional facilities, but also through your tireless work at FEGS, where you linked returning citizens with critical outpatient mental health services, and at the Brooklyn District Attorney's Office, where you helped shape community-based responses to justice. In each of these roles, you never broke the connection to NYS DOCS, always seeking to provide services for people transitioning from prison back to their communities.

You joined NYSMIC in its early stages of your career, and now you serve as a Board Member at Large of the New York State Minorities in Criminal Justice. It has been a privilege to share this organization with you and to witness your growth as a leader within it.

When I hosted NYSMICJ plenary sessions, first in 2012 and again in 2024, inviting you as a panelist was a "no-brainer." Your expertise, clarity, and ability to inspire left the audience in awe. You have always been able to translate principles of civil engagement into action for empowerment and change.

What pleases me most today is knowing you have gone on to direct the Criminal Justice Program at Kingsborough Community College. In that role, you are shaping the third and fourth generations of advocates for justice. You continue the struggle, ensuring it lives on and evolves for those who come after us. Be well as you continue in the Struggle for Justice.

Kim B. (Student & Colleague)

I met Vanda Seward in 2004 when she was my criminal justice professor at the College of New Rochelle. One day in class, I said of a man returning from prison, "He did his time. Now he's coming home. Let's see what happens from here." I think that was the moment Vanda really noticed me—and I've been grateful ever since.

At the time, I had just lost my job. Vanda asked me to submit my résumé and quickly arranged an interview. A few weeks later, I was working at FEGS as a forensic case manager. That was the start of a mentorship that changed my life. When I worked for her at FEGS Link, she saw strengths in me that I couldn't see in myself.

Vanda always went above and beyond. As a single parent, I struggled financially, and she made sure my daughter never went without—even at Christmas, when things were tight. She made sure there was always a gift under our tree. More than once, her voice of reason saved me, like the time I was ready to get physical with my police officer boyfriend to throw him out, and she firmly told me, "Kim, you cannot put your hands on him—he's the police. Call 911 and let them handle it."

When my daughter ran away to a friend's house, Vanda didn't hesitate. She called the mother and said, "If she's not home within the next hour, I'm sending the police to your door." An hour later, my daughter was home.

Vanda has been my mentor, friend, and even the reason I met the love of my life. Today, I'm thriving and a homeowner in North Carolina, and I know part of that is because of her support and belief in me. Vanda, I love you, and I can never thank you enough.

Donna H. (Friend/Comrade)

I first met Dr. Vanda Seward a year after my release from serving twenty-seven years in prison, when she was the Director of Reentry for New York State Parole. I reached out to her for help obtaining a travel pass so I could attend school out of state. At first, she thought I was asking for a travel agent referral—it was her staff who told her I was on parole.

Years later, Vanda still sees me as she sees everyone else: as someone she can call a friend. She exhibits a humanity rarely shown to justice-impacted people.

Loyce D. (Former NYS Department of Correctional Services Superintendent)

Vanda has been a consistent force for positive change in the criminal justice system, and I have had the privilege of knowing her for over 25 years. Although I can't pinpoint the exact moment our paths first crossed, I can say with certainty that over the years, our lives have intersected many times due to our shared passion for improving the system.

Before my retirement, we were both working on reentry initiatives, though we never had the opportunity to collaborate directly. As the Statewide Director of Transitional Services for NYSDOCS, I participated in meetings with the Kings County Reentry Task Force, which Vanda was leading. It quickly became clear to me that Vanda had assembled a dynamic and dedicated group of professionals and volunteers committed to providing essential resources for incarcerated individuals returning to society.

Vanda led these meetings with a perfect blend of sternness and kindness, always maintaining an air of professionalism that commanded respect, while ensuring everyone felt heard and valued. Her leadership created an environment where everyone knew their contributions were crucial to the group's success.

After I transitioned into a new role as Deputy Superintendent of Programs, I no longer worked directly in reentry, but Vanda and I stayed in touch, frequently connecting at conferences. It wasn't long before she took on a new role as the Statewide Director of Reentry Services for NYSDOCCS. Even though I no longer worked in the Central Office, we continued our discussions about the challenges and barriers to successful reentry, always sharing insights and strategies for overcoming the obstacles faced by incarcerated individuals.

Vanda has a unique presence that commands attention the moment she enters a room. She exudes authority with ease and can quickly make everyone feel like they are her newest friend. More than that, she has the expertise to back up every impression she leaves. Her ongoing educational pursuits only add to her impressive knowledge base, and I wouldn't be surprised if she is the smartest person in the room, wherever she goes.

Her leadership and commitment to reentry services have had a lasting impact, and I am grateful for the opportunity to have witnessed her work over the years.

Anthony D. (Advocacy Comrade)

One moment that has always stayed with me happened during a Brooklyn Monthly Reentry meeting. That morning, after hearing the repeated use of the words "inmate" and "offender" to describe my community, you literally walked up and down the aisle, calling it out for what it was: dehumanizing language that had no place among people committed to justice. You didn't just name it—you corrected it, with conviction and clarity. The room went silent. I remember thinking, Now that's speaking truth to power!

That moment spoke volumes about your integrity and moved me deeply. As for when we first met, the timeline may blur, but I always remember your spirit entering the space before your name did—centered, unflinching, and unapologetically rooted in truth.

Whether in meetings, corridors, or community gatherings, your presence has always been one of fierce advocacy and grounded purpose. I love your blackness. Thank you for letting me walk part of this journey with you. Blessings and power to you always, Sis.

Stacey D. (Colleague & Friend)

So many moments come to mind, but I always return to the beginning—your first day at the Manhattan parole office. I'll never forget it. I was wearing orange patent leather gator shoes, and you looked at me and said, "Dem shoes are fly." In that instant, I thought, This lady is going to be cool to work for.

That memory is just one piece of our friendship. The tears (always mine), the laughs, the jokes, and even the moments of anger (again, mine) will always stay with me. You've been my friend, teacher, confidant, and unwavering source of support—whether at school, work, or in my personal life. Love you, Seward!

Feleica R. (Colleague)

When I was attending the FEGS job readiness program in Lower Manhattan, you came to my class and asked for a volunteer to grade your students' exams. The instructor looked at me, and I volunteered. From that day on, whenever you had exams or needed help at the front desk, you would always call me.

When a receptionist position opened, you encouraged me to apply—and I got the job. Soon after, a position for an Entitlement Specialist became available. You pushed me to apply, even though I wasn't sure I could handle the responsibilities. I had only learned by observing and assisting case managers. With your guidance and the help of the former Entitlement Specialist, I mastered the role.

In that position, I began working closely with the forensic population—people returning home from jail or prison. I escorted clients to welfare and Social Security offices, helping them secure food stamps, cash benefits, and, most importantly, Medicaid for psychotropic medications. I'll never forget traveling in the rain with clients, determined to make sure they had what they needed. I loved that work.

When FEGS closed, I wasn't sure what would come next. I didn't have the same credentials as others, but I had the drive and experience. A position opened at CASES, serving the same population, and I became a Forensic Case Manager. My understanding of mental illness even helped me support a loved one who was recently diagnosed.

Looking back, I see how far I've come. If it weren't for you believing in me, I don't know where I'd be today. And to think—it all started with me volunteering to grade your students' exams. Thank you so much. Love ya.

Raquel A. (Broadway Playwright & Comrade)

Dr. Vanda Seward, you have been instrumental in my understanding of justice, service to impacted communities, using proximity to power to shift policy, and connection with folks as a liberatory practice.

I was drawn to how you create community, gathering parties from ends of the spectrum together to create change, how shifting narratives shift political perspectives, and end oppressive policies when we can view the full human, not just the parts rejected by society. Your genius is how you used your positionality to serve and influence in a variety of spaces where you shifted oppressive conditions through advocacy, teaching, and radical generosity.

Jackie O. (Former Student, Mentee, & Friend)

I first met you during my freshman year at the College of New Rochelle in the Bronx. At that time, I had no plans beyond finishing college. I still remember you walking into the room, introducing yourself, and me instantly wanting to be just like you. You didn't look like a typical professor, and I was captivated by your style, grace, and teaching. I ended up taking every class you taught, including the online courses (and I hated online classes, to be honest).

At the time, I worked at Harlem Hospital as a care aide on the psychiatric unit. As I became more focused on school, I decided I wanted to work in the criminal justice field as a counselor. When I told you this, you encouraged me to volunteer with justice-impacted youth to build my résumé. After graduation, I wanted to commit fully to the field but feared leaving my stable city job with good benefits. You asked my age and reminded me I had time to return to a pensioned position if needed. With your encouragement, I took the leap, resigned, and began working at the Osborne Association in the Bronx.

About a year later, I became an Offender Rehabilitation Coordinator (ORC) at Sing-Sing Correctional Facility, grateful to return to state service. Soon after, I was offered a position as an NYS Parole Officer. With three children under 18, I worried about managing the academy, but you—as always—told me to figure it out and reminded me I had a year before losing my ORC line.

Fifteen years later, I'm still here—not only loving my job as a Parole Officer but continuing to be inspired by you every day. You guided me through some of the hardest times in my life. You are not only my mentor but also my family, and I can't imagine where I'd be without you. Thank you for always believing in me. Love you always.

Kevin/Rondu M. (Bonus Brother & Comrade)

Shortly after I came home as a returning citizen, you gave me brutally honest advice. After I shared the details of my past and current relationships, you told me not to feel compelled to move to another state just because a woman I liked wanted me to follow her. You reminded me that I owed her nothing and that my focus should be on my own transition back into society after 28 years of incarceration.

You also advised me not to commit to a relationship with my daughter's mother unless I truly wanted to. You asked me hard but necessary questions: Do you want to be in a committed relationship? Are you in love with her? Do you want to relocate to Elizabeth, New Jersey, when all your connections are in the New York Tri-State area? This conversation happened during COVID, not long after my release on June 10, 2019.

I also remember your visit to me at Downstate Correctional Facility after I was transferred there from Rikers Island, having been found guilty of first- and second-degree robbery and sentenced to 25 years to life. That visit gave me the strength and motivation to face the uncertainty and harsh realities of the NYS DOCCS system. Years later, shortly after my release, you agreed to join my panel at Columbia University's Beyond the Bars Conference, alongside other leaders in justice-impacted work. My presentation, Authentic Reconciliation, was made even more powerful by your presence.

Lastly, I will never forget when you called to tell me you had taken your husband and lifelong partner, David Seward, to the hospital with extreme distress from COVID, and then called again to share the heartbreaking news of his passing. That moment stays with me.

Victor P. (Advocacy Comrade)

When I first met Dr. Vanda Seward, it was at the National Action Network headquarters in Harlem, NY, where the 2nd Chance Committee—of which I am a cofounder—was holding a re-entry meeting I was facilitating. She had approved her staff in the parole re-entry unit to send people to the support group meetings we established for those coming home from prison. Her staff member, Detrell, set everything up and began sending people to us.

That day, a woman came in, sat quietly at the back, and said nothing. The rest of us, me included, kept wondering who she was.

Eventually, I walked over, introduced myself, and asked her name. She replied, "My name is Dr. Vanda Seward, and I am the Statewide Director for the New York State Department of Corrections and Community Supervision." I just said, "Wow."

Years later, I'm still struck by the fact that she took the time to come to Harlem to see what we were doing—and came not as someone in charge but as an ordinary citizen, simply observing from the back.

She and I have built a strong relationship since. We call on each other for community-based events focused on prison and parole reform. Like many of us in advocacy, she is the voice and face of the voiceless and the weary.

For the past seven years, we've collaborated on developing a criminal justice session at Al Sharpton's

National Action Network annual conference, bringing in speakers from across the country for our panel discussions. When I think of people who worked at her level in NYS DOCCS or the district attorney's office, I don't usually imagine someone so down-to-earth—someone who rolls up their sleeves to do the hard work of advocacy.

Dr. Seward is deeply invested in reforming the criminal justice system—whether from within or while pushing from outside. She is about the work and about helping people impacted by the system.

Those of us directly affected by this system value her dedication. Vanda is someone you want on your side, in any environment. She doesn't just talk about it—she lives it.

Roger S. (Friend)

When I was released from prison in 2014, I remember going to the Brooklyn DA Office's ComALERT program and hearing someone mention your name—you were back at ComALERT. I was so happy. I thought, "Oh my God, Doc." It was such an emotional moment—not just for me, but for you too.

Another memory that stands out was celebrating your and Dave's 25th wedding anniversary, your retirement party (even though I didn't want you to retire), and later, standing with you during the loss of your husband. I was proud to be there, to share in those personal moments you allowed me into.

I'm grateful for how much you've helped me—and countless others—especially when I first came home not knowing anything. I didn't even know how to use a cell phone or navigate the train. You helped me with all of that, and it meant everything.

You've always had such patience with people, but at the same time, you never tolerated nonsense. I've admired that balance. I might hold back at times, but you'd say directly, "Don't come here with that." That's powerful. Over time, I realized that directness comes from years of working in corrections. In that environment, you couldn't afford to be soft—you had to stand tall and firm, especially as a woman, or people would try to take advantage. Yet even with that firmness, you always showed respect.

When I hear you're sick, I truly worry. I pray for you. Losing you would feel like losing an arm—that's how deeply your presence matters in my life.

And then there's the title of "Doctor." I remember when you didn't yet have it, when you just had your master's. Now you're Dr. Vanda Seward—and that title carries weight. It's not about money; it's about purpose. That same purpose shines every time we talk. You were made for this work—it's in you. That's why I respect you so much.

Eva G. (Colleague)

Almost twenty years ago, I was in the FEGS Welfare-to-Work program in the Bronx. I had just lost my job and applied for public assistance. You were the supervisor, and one day you needed help with something—I can't even remember what. You walked into the classroom, asked for a volunteer, and I raised my hand.

Not long after, you encouraged me to apply for a position at FEGS. I did—and I got the job.

When you later transferred to another division of FEGS in Manhattan, I was struggling with the director of my current program. You told me to apply for a role with your new team—the Entitlement Specialist position for the NYC LINK program. I knew nothing about mental health or working with people coming out of jails and prisons. But you mentored me. You taught me everything.

Then, when a case manager position opened, you encouraged me again. I thought that was it—I had a stable job with benefits to support my five children. I was content.

But you weren't done with me. You pushed me to go to college.

When I said I didn't have the time, you refused to accept it. You told me to go to the college, fill out the paperwork, and reminded me that I could do school during work time. You were serious—and I listened.

I followed your lead. I started my bachelor's degree, and you stayed with me. I remember sitting in my office, work done, chatting with colleagues, and you'd pass by and ask, "Everything finished? Then why aren't you doing homework? Don't you have reading for school?"

Even at lunch, you pushed me: "Read during lunchtime. You don't have time to play."

Before I knew it, I had my bachelor's degree. School became interesting. I enjoyed the journey so much that I went straight for my master's. And today, I have that master's.

Now, I'm the Assistant Director of a forensic unit with the Bowery Residents' Committee. What leadership, structure, and creativity do I bring to my team? I learned all of it from you. The way I manage and motivate my staff has drawn attention from my supervisors, and I keep growing.

None of this would have happened without you. You saw in me more than a case manager—more than just a mom. You set a higher standard for me, and because of you, I've set the same bar higher for my children.

I now have eleven children; all the older ones have graduated from high school, and one is a college graduate. They were motivated by watching what I became—and I became that because of you.

I never thought I'd love my job, but I now understand the passion you had for helping justice-impacted individuals and others whose situations didn't define them. Thank you— for believing in me, for pushing me, for seeing my potential before I could. I owe it all to you.

Lindsey A. (Craig Newmark Graduate School of Journalism Academic Advisor)

Dr. Vanda Seward—or Ms. Vanda, as I often call her out of deep respect—is a force. From the moment she joined our program, her presence was undeniable. As Director of Academic Affairs, I've reviewed many student backgrounds, but hers stood out. I remember thinking, "Now she wants to be a journalist? This woman wants to do everything!" And she did!!

Ms. Vanda walked into our J-School newsroom and commanded respect without saying a word. She knew exactly who she was and what she came to accomplish. Students see her not just as a peer, but as a mentor.

Every advising session with her began with a plan and ended with a life lesson. When she told me she wanted to write for the Amsterdam News, I connected her with someone. She didn't just get one byline—but became an Op-Ed Contributor. That IS Dr. Vanda Seward: driven, ambitious, focused, and always pushing the bar higher.

Working with her has been a true privilege—she inspires those around her, including me.

As I gathered these reflections, I realized they weren't just memories—they were mirrors. Each voice revealed how others have experienced me, how I've shown up in their lives, and how our paths have shaped one another. These aren't just acknowledgments; they're affirmations of purpose, resilience, and connection.

Their words reminded me that while I've poured into others, I've also been poured into—through love, loyalty, and truth. These voices have grounded me, especially in moments when I questioned my impact. Legacy isn't just about what we leave behind—it's about how we live, love, and lift others while we're here.

To everyone who shared their truth with me: thank you. Your words are part of this story, and your presence is forever part of my journey.

Opening My Heart Again

I threw myself into work, reentry, policy, and advocacy, believing purpose might fill the empty spaces. But healing isn't linear—and neither is love. One day, with more curiosity than I expected, I picked up my phone, opened a dating app, and swiped. Left. Left. Left. And then… right.

After 28 years of marriage, after losing my husband, I knew David was the last OG in my life. He had a standard. No one could measure up. So, when I finally considered dating again, I knew one thing for sure: I wasn't looking for anyone from the streets or still tied to them. That chapter was closed. I remembered watching Ready to Love and Tommy telling the singles to start dating someone outside their "type."

People kept talking about dating apps—the new way to meet people. At first, I brushed it off. But curiosity crept in. After some thought (and a little side-eye at my own hesitation), I decided to try. Before I did, I sat down with my daughters, Tanika & Tyra. I wanted them to hear it from me: "I'm thinking about dating again." They gave me the green light, with love and support.

So, I created a profile on a Black dating site. I was clear: mature, emotionally intelligent, spiritually grounded, 50–60 age range. I wasn't asking for Idris Elba—just someone with his life together.

Let's just say… the pickings were slim.

Some profile pictures looked like they were taken in 1998 on a flip phone. Others looked like mugshots. The first conversations? Dry as toast. The real deal-breaker? How many men in that age group had serious medical issues, I don't know why I expected different—but I did.

One man told me on our first date that he'd had five strokes in two years. Another pulled out his glucose monitor at the dinner table and tested his sugar right in front of me. I wasn't judging, but I was blinking in disbelief.

I went on three dates in total. None were terrible, but none were memorable either. They felt more like errands than encounters—something to do, not someone to know. The third man was a realtor at an elite firm, considering becoming a pastor. He was kind and respectful, but our conversations were painfully dry. Nice man, but no spark.

After that, I hit pause. I needed to step back and breathe.

So, I did what I should have done from the start: I talked to God.

I said, "Lord, I want different—no street ties. No drama. No negative energy. Calm. Laid-back. No smoking, no drinking, and please, limited to no medical concerns. Not in my original age range. Maybe a little younger, a little healthier."

Soon after, I logged back into the app and saw a man who looked vibrant. His profile said he was sixty. I sent him a message: "You look good for your age—what's your secret?"

He replied, "That's a typo." I laughed.

That one message turned into a two-hour text conversation. He was surprised at how fast I texted—he thought I was using a keyboard. I learned that English was his second language, and he used a translator to read my messages. His first language was French, and he had only been in the U.S. for six years. Still, his English was impressive. I asked, "Do you have a French accent?" He said, "I don't know." I laughed again.

Naturally, I wondered if he was looking for citizenship. But before I could ask, he told me he had been a U.S. citizen for two years. He seemed to answer questions before I could even voice them.

Everything I had asked God for, Lewis had.

He came from a humble, educated family in Gabon, Central Africa. His father was a retired school principal, his mother a teacher, and all his sisters were college graduates. When I asked if he had gone to college, he said no—because watching his sisters, he decided it wasn't worth it. They were always broke and asked him for money. I told him he wasn't alone in that way of thinking; many people feel the same.

Lewis works a steady job and runs his own business, Lewis West Harlem Driving Lessons, which is growing steadily. I helped where I could, though I knew little about the driving school world.

At first, we had our hiccups, like most new relationships. I'm expressive, verbal, and yes, I can curse like a sailor. I'm carefree and allergic to drama. Lewis is quiet, thoughtful, and doesn't speak just to fill the silence. When he's deep in thought about home, family, or finances, he goes inward. And anyone who knows me knows there's nothing quiet about me.

But over time, we adjusted. I try not to curse as much, and he's learned to open up more when something's on his mind. We respect each other's careers and goals. He's said he has learned more about the criminal justice system from me than he ever imagined. And even though he doesn't like big social settings, he has attended a few criminal justice events with me.

We've shared the holidays, which is new to him. Back home in Africa, he didn't celebrate Christmas or birthdays— but now he celebrates with me. My daughter and I are Christmas fanatics, so it's hard to avoid. We've even traveled to France together, although we went in the winter and it was cold as heck. He took me sightseeing, shopping, and showed me where he used to live. Everyone who knows me knows I do not like cold weather, but between being happy to go abroad and shop, I bundled up, layers on, and went out anyway. Between sampling perfumes and spotting every Louis Vuitton store, I forgot it was cold.

Being new to America and New York City, Lewis makes going out exciting because he sees NYC through a different lens than I do—as someone born and raised here. He's amazed that I can drive through most of the five boroughs without a GPS.

He's not a huge fan of dining out, but he'll go because he knows that's my thing. He prefers home-cooked meals, which I don't mind. He even taught me how to cook rice properly. He said mine was tasteless and hard. I fry fish for him without cornmeal or batter, and yes—the head stays on. My grandmother used to fry fish the same way, and when I was little, I'd poke the eye with a fork while it was frying. She always knew because the fisheye would be dry when she ate it. Nasty, I know.

We're going strong four years together now, and we're each other's biggest cheerleaders. Whenever one of us starts something new, the other is right there rooting. Lewis and my daughter both tell me, "You need to sit down somewhere—you do too much."

I just smile and say, "I'll sit when I'm tired. I am retired, but not tired."

One thing I deeply appreciate is how he respects my relationship with my in-laws. That means everything to me. He has even said he's never seen anyone maintain such a close bond with their in-laws after losing a spouse. We're still family—nothing changes that. I would love for him to meet them one day, but he's hesitant. I respect that. It's not a requirement, but it would be nice.

I don't know where this relationship will go. But if it stays right here—no headaches, no stress, just love—I'm good.

The work continues to call me, in all its forms. Whether it's advocating for justice, supporting my family, or opening my heart to new love, I keep showing up. Because that's who I am. That's who I've always been. And that's who I'll continue to be.

Chapter 16
The Legacy I'm Still Writing

In My God's Hands—Retired, Not Tired; Still Called to Justice

"Retirement didn't end my calling—it expanded it. Justice isn't a job; it's a lifelong assignment, and I'm still reporting for duty."

Every lesson from my childhood shaped who I became: my mother's quiet strength and resourcefulness, the Methadone Clinic where I learned that people are people regardless of circumstance, and Boobie's street wisdom about being your brother's keeper while staying in control. Those early experiences taught me to see humanity in everyone, to speak truth without tearing others down, and to build unshakable loyalty with those who deserve it. God continues to bless me as I walk this path, educating, supporting, and using my voice for those unheard or misunderstood. I am giving my all and living my truth, 100%.

Seven years after retiring, I remain deeply engaged in advocacy. Without a gag order, I can finally speak freely about my experiences in the New York State Department of

Corrections and Community Supervision. Still, I do not disparage the agencies I worked for. I speak the truth. Criticizing the system alone does not create change; action does. Many high-level government employees remain silent out of fear of losing income or status. I never carried that fear. My pension is spread across city and state service; no single agency controls my livelihood.

My focus is on change, collaboration, and empowering others. I refuse to waste time gossiping or tearing people down. Many people do not know better until someone shows them. If you are not willing to offer that truth, then do not join the judgment. Supporting others, especially the formerly incarcerated, has always been part of my journey.

That one personal essay assignment in that Features Writing course at the Craig Newmark Graduate School of Journalism at CUNY, taught by Linda Villarosa, a renowned journalist and former executive editor of Essence, validated my life's journey. The validation from someone of her caliber, who is what I would call an unusual suspect, made me realize that my story, our stories—matter in ways I am still discovering.

My legacy is far from finished; it is being written every day I choose to speak truth, every person I mentor, every system I challenge, and every heart I help open to love again. The pen is still in my hand, and many more chapters lie ahead.

Life Is a Journey
We Don't Get to Quit…

Life is funny. Sometimes we are up on top of the mountain, soaring high, and other times, the struggle, the struggle is oh so real, it makes you want to cry.

Often, we battle against the here and now, against the desires of our hearts. We move forward not knowing what lies ahead; consequences are a shadow in the dark.

Our choices find us engulfed in a struggle; others come just to see if we weather the tide. Determination sets in, I won't be a victim, for I am a winner, I will overcome with inner drive.

Naysayers, fueling doubts, disappointments, even close family questions, what next? From deep inside, there's a calling, a resilience saying you can do this, it's just a test. Strapped by her bootstrings, a fight from the gut, a vision of a brighter future unfolds. It's no longer just about her or the naysayers; it's about a legacy soon to be told. A can do, a will do, with a nothing can stop me attitude; look out world, I can do anything.

You see, I have learned, what God has for you, for me, for mine, is ours for the grabbing. So, hold on and grab hold of the promise for your life, one set while still in the womb. The promise is that if you stay true to the creator and self, where you are planted, you will bloom. Who would have imagined this? Not making it out of high school, a teenage Mom, would go on to receive her diploma and her college degree, while taking life in her palm.

Let's not forget her Master's, Doctorate, Tenured Professor, and Radio host, as well. Surviving, no thriving against all odds, surpassing every statistic, they all were dispelled. She is a Black woman, a survivor; she has weathered some storms, sure, without regrets.

She's seen immeasurable growth, absolutely, just look at her journey, and let's not forget, this woman redefined with passion and determination what a Black woman looks like. A Black woman who has been in the trenches, who has lost and gained, and still fights. A Black woman who has never learned the meaning of no, you can't, it's over, just quit.

This Nubian Queen is an extraordinary woman, fearless, powerful, and full of grit. In her own right, this Black woman rose against all odds, and so can you. If you remember, life is a journey with choices, and the choice is truly up to you.

Inspirations from The Heart by Cheryl Lynn Iszard, © October 9, 2025.

Armor & Grace, What I Gave A… About

EARLY YEARS – SURVIVAL MODE (Teen Motherhood)

"Back then, 'I don't give a… wasn't about being hard. It was armor. When the world kept calling me a statistic, I stopped explaining myself. I wasn't reckless—I was protecting what was mine."

PROFESSIONAL LIFE – WORKING IN PRISONS / SYSTEMS

"In that environment, you either lose yourself—or draw the line. My line was clear: I don't give a ... about gossip, fake alliances, or chasing titles. I came to do the work, not play the game."

LOVE & FAMILY – MARRYING DAVID / RAISING A FAMILY

"People whispered when they found out I was marrying a man in green. But loving David taught me what I do and don't give a ...about. I chose us, and that was enough."

CAREER EVOLUTION – ADVOCACY & REENTRY WORK

"By the time I was building programs for the formerly incarcerated, my 'I don't give a ...' had matured. It wasn't about resistance—it was about focus. I wasn't here for popularity. I was here to build."

POST-RETIREMENT – SPEAKING OUT

"Retirement gave me freedom. No more gag orders. No more pretending. I don't give a ... about being palatable. I give a .... about the truth."

FINAL CHAPTER – *"I Don't Give ... A Final Reflection"*

"I've said it all my life—but now I say it with peace. I don't give a ... isn't about not caring. It's about caring deeply for the right things—my joy, my legacy, my truth. Everything else? Let it go."

Acknowledgements

This story may carry my name, but it was built on the strength, sacrifice, and love of many.

To my late husband, David: thank you for thirty years of loving me fully and fearlessly. Our journey was unexpected yet genuine, rooted in loyalty. Even in your absence, your spirit steadies me. This book is part of your legacy.

To my mother, Audrey, and my grandmother, Hortense (rest in peace): your strength and insistence on education gave me the foundation I needed to rise. You modeled resilience. I stand firmly on what you built, and I am forever grateful.

To my daughter, Tanika — "The Prize," my little Black girl: thank you for growing with me and giving my life direction when I needed it most. You were never a burden— only a blessing. Watching you become a poised, graceful, compassionate Black woman and mother has been my greatest joy and proudest accomplishment.

To my brother, even as life took us down different paths. You may never have imagined this would become my story, but you are part of it.

To my sweetie, Lewis: thank you for showing up quietly, consistently, and with patience. Your patience gave me space to write, reflect, and breathe. This memoir exists because of your steady support.

Boobie, whose spirit lives on, and the Crew—you were my early teachers and anchors. You reminded me I was never alone.

To the people I've worked with inside correctional facilities, in reentry programs, nonprofits, across New York State, and City—though I cannot name you because of active affiliations with NYSDOCCS, thank you for your honesty, courage, and trust. You remind me why this work matters.

To all individuals impacted by the criminal legal system: thank you for allowing me to witness and carry your stories. You are the reason I fight, teach, write, and refuse to be silent.

To my mentors and public school teachers: thank you for seeing more in me than my circumstances. Your belief helped me imagine a future far beyond what statistics predicted.

And finally, to the younger me—the teenage mother, the rebel, the seeker—thank you for not giving up. You were enough then, and you are enough now. Your grit and fire made all of this possible.

www.ingramcontent.com/pod-product-compliance
Lightning Source LLC
Chambersburg PA
CBHW060344310726
48976CB00003B/713